CORRUPT ME
IMMORTAL VICES AND VIRTUES BOOK 8

EVERLY FROST

CORRUPT ME
Everly Frost

Copyright © 2022 by Everly Frost

Immortal Vices and Virtues Universe Copyright © 2022 Kel Carpenter
LLC.

Cover design by Yocla Designs

All rights reserved.

Earth has changed.

Over several thousand years, portals opened up all over the world, each one leading to a different realm with different magic.

Supernatural creatures crossed over to Earth through the portals, and magic from the realms bled into humans over time.

Houses were formed.
Battles were fought.
Blood was spilled.

Peace between the Houses was hard-won.

Now, all the world has magic.

But magic can be a curse.

And so the threads of fate continue to weave...

CHAPTER 1
SLATER

I'm all out of options.

The desert wind plucks at my wings, a hot gust knocking me down toward the endless sand dunes that stretch in every direction. My bird-shaped shadow looms up at me as the wind threatens to drive me into the scorching sand while I fight to remain airborne.

I've stayed in my raven form for the last five days. Five long, sweltering days with nothing but golden sand below me and a clear sky above me. Freezing at night. Boiling during the day. Somehow, I'm still alive, but I won't be for long.

This harsh environment will end me.

The horizon blurs and shimmers, and the only thing that keeps me flying is the tendril of magic I'm following.

It's become a lifeline, a bright spark in the darkness overtaking my mind.

A fucking *deceptive* bright spark because it will almost certainly lead to my death.

But hell, I don't have a choice.

I've been cursed.

The dark magic that is stealing my life away is evident in the three white feathers standing out among the otherwise inky plumage on my right wing.

My only hope is a secretive coven of three witches who answer to no one and won't appreciate my intrusion. It's taken me months to track the thread of their magic. Along the way, I've encountered nearly every kind of witch and each of them told me the same thing: They can't help me. Not with the curse. Certainly not with finding the reclusive coven of witches who might have the power to save my life.

I lost count of the times I was told: *"Give up. Better to die cursed than to face the wrath of the Maiden, the Mother, and the Crone."*

I wouldn't give up. Not least because my fucking pride wouldn't let me. I'm an expert in tracking the untraceable, and I refused to accept that three witches could evade me.

Then seven weeks ago, I finally sensed the distinctly sharp energy of powerful witches traveling together. I was in Portland at the time, in the headquarters of the House of Fire and Fluorite. It was a dangerous place for me to be since I hadn't been invited into their territory and that House has been in turmoil for some time now.

Luckily for me, when I'm in raven form, I don't cast an aura. I can soar right across territory lines unobserved, which has made me invaluable to the House of Gold and Garnet, a House of mercenaries. Being able to blend into the shadows while tracking a target comes in handy in my line of work.

The thread of magic I'm now following is faint and skillfully concealed, the finest of filaments consisting of three distinct magics wound around each other. It led me here to the vast Sahara desert.

Each of their magics warns me that their power is beyond compare.

If I find them, they'll most likely kill me.

If I *don't* find them... well... the curse will finish me.

Fucking awesome choices.

As the desert wind plucks at me again, I'm increasingly aware that I won't last much longer. Taking my raven form was tactical—not only can I travel faster, but I can survive in this form for longer without food or water. But not forever.

My raven's talons cling to the only belongings I brought with me into the desert. I started off with a small satchel containing water, food, a phone, and a pair of boxers so I wouldn't be forced to walk around naked when I shifted back into my human form.

I don't carry jewelry or an object adorned with a stone representing my House. In Gold and Garnet, we favor tattoos, particularly because jewels can catch the light and betray our location.

Twenty-five years ago, when the Houses went to war in a battle that came to be known as the Great Sacrifice, my family was wiped out. Vesperus, the former King of Gold and Garnet, took me in when I had nowhere else to go. Sure, he saw my potential, but his heart is honorable.

He could have killed me. Instead, he gave me a home.

Now, the new Gold and Garnet King, Kaspian, has my faith and trust. I consider him, and his top assassin, the archangel Nolan, to be my brothers.

I wear my dagger-shaped tattoo across my heart as a mark of my loyalty to my House.

As for my supplies, my weakening state demanded that I ditch everything heavy.

Once I drank my last ration of water, I sent Kaspian a final text message. I let him know I was still searching. I didn't tell him that I might not remain alive much longer. If I gave him even a hint that I was in dire trouble, he'd send someone after me, and I won't risk anyone else's life in the pursuit of these witches.

After that, I pared down my luggage to my boxers.

Now, I'm not even sure I need those.

My dignity is losing priority to my need to conserve energy.

I convince myself I have one more day of life in me, and I ignore the fact that it's probably more like one more hour.

The weaker I grow, the brighter the white feathers on my wing appear, their ivory color even more brilliant in the sunlight reflected off the sand.

I have no fucking idea how the curse happened. Or why I was cursed. I only know *when* and *where*.

I was tracking an unknown magical entity that had slipped through one of the portals. I located the strange entity in an old pub in Dublin. The last thing I remember was prowling across the street outside the pub, intending to go inside. My hand had connected with the front door, and then...

I have only snatches of memory.

Exploding glass and wood and bricks.

The *crunch* of my bones as the impact of the explosion and the weight of rubble bore down on me.

A brief instinct to take raven form and fly, but it was already too late.

I experienced a sharp pain like a needle of power piercing my heart, and then I lost consciousness.

I awoke to find a witch named Trixie fussing over me, a deep worry in her vibrant, blue eyes. I waved her away, not only because I felt fine, but because her healing magic had felt weirdly abrasive. Like my body was rejecting it.

Clearly miffed, she announced that she couldn't cure the kind of darkness that had taken over me.

"You've lost all your light," she warned me.

Now, I experience a pang of regret at the memory of how blithely I dismissed her concerns.

As it turned out, the magical entity I was tracking had nothing to do with my curse.

But all too soon, it became apparent that Trixie was right.

I lost my light, and now darkness is swamping me, clouding my thoughts, hindering my reason. The harder I push back against it, the more aggressive it becomes.

I used to believe that I could survive anything. Evade any threat. My ability to shift into the form of a raven gave me anonymity and allowed me to move in the shadows. I worked hard and proved my loyalty to my House.

I wanted nothing but the chance to prove myself.

None of that seems to matter now.

In the distance, the sand dunes appear a little less even. The bumpy formations give me a burst of hope that I might finally reach my destination, until my raven's sharp eyesight confirms it's simply rubble.

If there were buildings there once, they're gone now. A fucking mirage to give me false hope.

The desert wind billows up around me and I'm forced to acknowledge that my time is up. The tendril of magic stretches into the distance and I'll never make it to its source.

Darkness encroaches on the edges of my raven's vision, shadows extend across the golden landscape like clawed fingers stretching toward me, and an icy sensation strangles my heart.

I'm suddenly struck with a sense that death might only be the beginning.

Something's shifting within my mind.

I can barely breathe as my raven's chest squeezes and his wings fail to beat.

As I plummet toward the sand, I'm not sure who or what I'm becoming.

CHAPTER 2

EMMALINE

Asudden blast of hot air hits my cheeks.

I pause in the middle of pressing a belladonna seed into a pot of moist soil. My focus flashes across my garden to the doorway in the stone wall on the far side—the direction from which the gust of wind came.

An *impossible* gust of wind.

The desert air doesn't pass into our haven. Or, rather, it *shouldn't*.

We live in the center of the Sahara near one of the major portals—the one leading to the world of witches.

From the outside, our home looks like nothing more than the remnants of a crumbling, sandstone structure. Anyone who makes it this far into the desert would dismiss the few collapsed walls as rubble. They would pass by, unaware that stepping through the only intact doorway in the crumbling wall would lead them into an oasis.

My garden.

It's the one place where I can feel truly at peace.

Smoothing down my white, linen dress, I retrieve my house ring from the little wooden table I use for potting plants and herbs. The sapphire set atop the ring glints as I pull it onto my left ring finger. The stone is evidence that I belong to the House of Spirit and Sapphire. Not all members choose to wear a ring; some place a sapphire on another object they carry with them.

The other two witches in my coven wear their House rings on their right hand, but my right hand is already adorned. A wide, lace bracelet sits around my right wrist. A silver chain extends from the bracelet down the back of my hand to a pearlescent ring on my forefinger. All three pieces—the bracelet, chain, and pearl ring—are magically protected from the dirt I was just burying my hands in.

They are pure. Like me.

In this world, the strength of a witch's magic is given labels. Crones are the most powerful, mothers are some-where in the middle, and maidens have mild magic.

In my coven, things are different.

We are a coven of three witches and have taken pains to keep our existence and location a secret. Some who have heard whispers about us call us 'The Triarchy.' Others call us 'The Coven of Three.' I'm sure we have other names, but to our House leaders, we are simply 'The Three.'

The Crone is a mistress of illusion, and she created this place to protect and conceal us. She wears a glamour to conceal her natural features, which are too ghastly for other supernaturals to behold.

The Mother is a mistress of destiny who weaves a tapestry made up of the threads of fate. Every supernatural, living and dead, has a place in her tapestry. But more importantly, she can identify the pivotal moments along a thread where a person's fate can be changed one way or another.

Then there's me.

I swivel to the part of the garden behind me that contains a small waterfall that drops tranquilly into a grotto. That waterfall is another illusion hiding a second layer of building within our home.

A castle sits behind it, unseen from this side.

Within the castle, the Crone and the Mother are busy deciding the next move we'll make in the fate they're weaving for this world.

In our haven, time behaves differently. It's slower, allowing the Crone and the Mother to check and consider their next moves carefully before acting.

Nothing is done in haste.

They don't involve me in their machinations, and I've learned not to ask questions. I've been taught my place. Sometimes, they have to make 'difficult' decisions and my hands are to remain pure of those.

I, too, have a role to play.

For every dark deed, I am the light—the pure force— that maintains balance so fate never tips too far one way or the other.

Evil and good. Dark and light. Pain and hope.

Violence and peace. If ever fate is in danger of tipping too far in the wrong direction, I am the protective force that brings it back.

Even the belladonna seed I was planting has transformed at my touch, sprouting from a poisonous seed into a miniature sunflower.

I press my fingertips to my cheek, where the hot air slapped me like a hand demanding my attention. There's no way I can ignore the gust of wind, not when it defied all of the magical securities that The Crone has placed around our home.

In fact, it makes me wonder if something could be very wrong with those protections.

Just as I consider hurrying to the castle to warn my sisters, the same gust of hot air that slapped me in the face forms a tiny whirlwind right in front of me.

It rips apart the sunflower, scattering its petals across the table like a child throwing a tantrum to secure my attention.

The gust rises up and swirls around me, causing a chill to travel down my spine despite the heat in the air. Rushing up around my face, the gust plucks at my long, brown hair, pulling the strands in the direction of the far door to the desert beyond our haven.

Whatever is causing this gust won't wait for me to run back to the castle for advice.

I hurry toward the door, striding along the mossy path that curves around lush bushes and rare plants from which I make my potions.

The path curves in the middle to accommodate the

largest tree in my garden, a weeping willow with sweeping fronds that descend to the ground in elegant strands. Its drooping foliage is decorated with what looks like random pieces of cloth, beads, and charms—but that is only the external fronds.

Like other aspects of my home, the tree also has layers of illusion around it.

Beneath the external layer of fronds lies a deeper layer, onto which are tied magical objects that have, through some twist of fate, been lost to their owners.

I have a knack for sensing lost things and finding them, and my power allows me to cast protection spells over them.

Some objects contain immense power and must be protected. Others hold only sentimental value. The Crone continues to tell me to abandon those, but I refuse. The power of the object is not in its material value, but in its emotional value to the person who owned it.

There is power in heart.

I hurry along the path beside the Tree of Lost Things, but I pull up sharply before I pass it completely.

Wait a minute...

I defy the gust of wind, which continues to pluck at my dress and hair, while I take a step back to peer at three objects hanging from external fronds.

Three black feathers.

They weren't here this morning.

I immediately recognize them as raven feathers.

But how did they get here? And why?

It's not the first time an object has appeared on its

own, as if it were seeking safe haven from the world outside.

Recently, an object of great power startled me by appearing on the outer fronds of the tree. I immediately acted to keep it safe, casting a protective spell around it to hide its presence. While the Crone can cast powerful protections, my ability in that regard is limited to concealing the true nature of a thing. It seems to go hand in hand with my ability to find lost items—I can also protect them. Usually, I do this by placing them on the Tree of Lost Things, but in the case of that powerful object, I kept it close to me.

I also kept its presence a secret from the Crone and the Mother because they would not have been able to pass up the chance to harness its power for their own ends.

Sky Serpell, a high-ranking member of my House with gorgeous, pink hair, came in search of that object with a tall, dark-haired shape-shifter named Zey.

I was glad to give the object back to them. My purpose in protecting any lost object is to return it to its rightful—or worthy—owner.

Sky and Zey lingered, and I could tell Sky had questions for me. Not only about the object, but about me and my coven. Her eyes were filled with curiosity, but despite her reputation as one of the most resilient members of my House, it wasn't safe for them to stay. In another life, Sky and I might have been friends. But I urged them to leave as quicky as possible.

The Crone and the Mother don't tolerate random visitors, all of whom are classed as invaders in their eyes.

Invaders are killed on sight.

Luckily, the Crone and the Mother were deep within the castle at the time and Sky and Zey escaped without any issues.

Only Odin, the god and male leader of our House, and Lady Gabriella, the archangel who is the female leader of our House, are permitted to visit us, although they don't like stepping foot here. And they rarely need to. They have other formidable witches and warlocks at their side—Reginald Reyes, a powerful warlock, to name one.

The Crone and the Mother made it clear to our House leaders that, while we are a part of the House of Spirit and Sapphire, we are to be left alone.

For some reason, Odin and Gabriella agreed to leave us be.

It might have had something to do with the thread of Odin's fate that the Mother was threatening to cut at the time.

Or possibly the way the Crone had removed her glamour and glowered at the both of them with her natural eyes. I've never met a single supernatural who didn't cower when pinned in her unfettered glare.

I think of Odin now as I study the three feathers.

He can communicate with ravens and has used them in the past to send us messages, so he doesn't have to speak to us directly.

My only explanation for the appearance of the

feathers—and the gust of air urging me toward the garden's entrance—is that Odin must be trying to communicate with us through his ravens.

But perhaps something has gone terribly wrong.

I reach for the feathers without thinking, only to gasp at the heat beating off them. It's scorching. So hot, it feels like a physical force colliding with my palm. At the same time, shadows play around the feathers despite the clear sky above me, the dark light jumping at my presence, as if it's trying to close the gap between us.

Quickly, I withdraw my hand, and the shadows settle back around the feathers.

I'm not sure what's going on here, but I try to catch my breath and calm my pounding heart before I hurry onward.

Reaching the door, I press my hand against it, bracing for what lies outside.

Even when I open the door, the protection around this place should keep the hot desert air at bay, but if I step beyond it, I'll be subjected to the harsh environment outside.

My palm tingles against the wooden surface and the hairs on the back of my neck stand on end.

I nearly jolt backward.

Something very dark is coming this way.

CHAPTER 3
EMMALINE

P ower stirs my heart to beat harder.

Pushing away my rising anxiety, I shove at the door, putting my shoulder against it to move the heavy wood through the sand beyond it. It makes a loud, grating sound as it rasps across the desert floor.

The moment the door is fully open, the desert wind rushes around me in full force, defying the protective barrier to wrap around my form and drag me the final step outside.

I gasp when my hair whips against my face, obscuring my view, and the full force of the sun beats down on me.

It's hot enough to make me want to curse.

As I pull my hair away from my face, what really gets my attention is the line of power glowing brightly across the air on my right.

It's made of three combined threads that look like threads of fate—the ones that the Mother weaves. Except that these ones aren't sitting in their rightful places in her tapestry. They're stretching from the doorway above my head and out across the desert, twined around each other to form a single thread.

The combined thread ends in the far distance, where a black bird flies.

The bird isn't much more than a blob, but I make out the shape of its wings.

It must be a raven.

But why are three threads of fate extended out across this desolate place to its location?

The bird is descending rapidly, being thrown around in the wind and pushed closer to the dunes with every gust, as if the wind wants to bash the poor creature against the gritty sand.

If it's dragged across the dunes at that velocity, its feathers will be ripped off.

For a second, I wonder if that might have already occurred, because it could explain how the three feathers appeared on my tree. Ripped off and perhaps carried inside by the first hot gust of wind.

Well, whatever's going on here, I'm not standing by while the bird dies.

Death may be something that the Crone and the Mother accept, and sometimes even orchestrate, but not me.

I take off across the hot sand, hitching up the folds of my white, linen dress and running as fast as I can while the surface burns the soles of my bare feet. I rarely wear shoes in my garden because of all the moss-lined surfaces, and I'm severely regretting that now.

It's too late to go back.

I follow the combined thread of magic as I push across the dunes. Luckily, the sand is flat enough here to make it a straight run and the magical thread isn't much higher than my head, so I don't need to crane my head too much to follow it.

The gap between me and the bird is closing rapidly, its flight bringing it toward me while I race closer to it.

I can finally make out details in its shape and the breadth of its wings, larger than most ravens but proportionate to its body. Startlingly, there's a patch of white on the underside of its right wing, which is very unusual. None of Odin's ravens have this trait.

It's flying low to the sand dunes now, its wings struggling to keep it aloft, its flight path erratic. I'm not close enough to see its eyes—and even then, it would be difficult to tell—but I suddenly wonder if it sees me.

If it doesn't, then I need to take care. The raven's sharp beak could take a chunk out of me.

It's still a good fifty paces away, so I jump to the side, out of its path, and crouch in the sand, gasping at the heat thrumming through my legs.

My dilemma now is that I don't want it to crash into the sand, but the bird isn't exactly going to alight politely in front of me.

It must be completely disoriented. Maybe even crazed from the desert heat. It should have seen me by now, but it gives no indication that it has.

Somehow, I have to stop it before it plummets into

the dunes and, unfortunately, my magic doesn't allow me to reach out across the air and physically grab it.

My powers are all oriented toward finding, retrieving, and protecting lost things. I can sense a lost item, create a temporary portal between me and the object—but not without a cost to myself—and call the object to me. All from the safety of my home, although the portal is large enough for me to step through if I need to. Then I can cast a concealment spell over the object.

I can also make a mean potion.

None of that seems particularly useful here.

Unless...

If the raven is lost, then my ability to call lost things to me might work on it even at this close range. It's a stretch, but it's the only option I have.

Taking a chance, I close my eyes and empty my mind of everything except the sharp pang of pain I feel in my heart when a lost thing calls to me.

I call within my mind, the invitation I make to every lost object.

Show yourself to me. I'll bring you home.

I gasp at the force that rushes over me.

Within my mind, the raven is a dark form, blurred at the edges. An inky cloud surrounds it, masking its true nature. Its dark eyes are like shining gems that dare me to call it closer.

A trickle of determination urges me to take it up on that dare.

I inhale deeply, my senses buzzing as if every part of my body is suddenly alive, feeling more than the hot air and the gritty granules beneath my feet. The ruffle of my dress against my chest and thighs. The heat across my lips, tingling at the edges of my mouth and along my jaw, whispering down the curve of my neck. Brushing across the tops of my breasts.

Bring yourself to me.

As my mental cry forms, my power extends beyond me, but then—

The glittering thread of magical fates that led me to the raven strikes inward, smacking into the tendril of my magic and cutting through it.

My magic disintegrates.

My eyes fly open. *What the—?*

The bird is only ten paces away from reaching my location, still flying low, but now the thread of fates whips back toward the bird as sharply as it cut through my magic.

Like a snake, it strikes at the raven's neck.

It wraps around the bird's throat, as if it would strangle the raven midair before it pulls it toward the sand.

"No!" My cry is plucked away into the air.

Somehow, I've caused this, but it wasn't my intention.

I'm on my feet and running forward, trying to reach the bird before it hits the sand, intending to throw myself beneath it to cushion its fall. Then, somehow, I'll deal with the fates wrapped around its neck.

I've only made it a few paces when the bird trans-forms mid-fall.

Its wings wrap back across its body, its chest expands,

and its talons extend. Its body is like a puzzle piece folding and expanding in two mere blinks until it's no longer a bird.

A man hits the dunes, every glistening muscle tensed, his enormous biceps bulging where he grips the thread of fates around his neck, no doubt attempting to keep the magical rope from cutting through his throat.

He's a shifter!

Even as I berate myself for not sensing his true nature before now, I continue to run toward him, hitching my dress up around my thighs to move faster.

He's fallen at an angle that puts him perpendicular to my position, and although he struggles to hold the threads of fate at bay, he turns his head toward me.

He's tanned and completely naked, every chiseled muscle of his chest, arms, and thighs glistening against the backdrop of the sand he's lying on, his elbows and heels digging turrets as he snarls against the restraint around his neck.

A tattoo sits across his left pectoral muscle and extends up the left side of his neck—the side I can see. The tattoo is shaped like a dagger. Or maybe a talon.

I have no doubt that he sees me now.

As I approach, more carefully now, he looks up at me through the strands of his hair with slate-gray eyes that are flecked with onyx.

Glittering flecks like black diamonds across a bed of stone.

There's a warning in his angry gaze, a threat that makes me shiver, but... not in fear.

My heart pounds rapidly as I stop beside him, my dress still scrunched up around my thighs and my hair billowing across my shoulders.

All I can manage is, "You aren't the raven I was expecting."

CHAPTER 4

SLATER

Her voice... *Fuck.*

It stops the breath in my chest.

Ethereal. Otherworldly. Neither descriptor comes close to the magic that seems to steal around each word she forms with her mouth. A mouth I'm suddenly focused on despite my desperate need to escape the tightening magic looped around my neck.

Before the thread struck me, my sight had gone completely dark.

I couldn't see where I was going. I didn't know if death had already taken me.

I was certain I was about to hit the sand dunes when magic of a kind I couldn't identify reached across the darkness and latched on to me.

"Show yourself to me. I'll bring you home."

It was a command I wanted to obey. My raven practically burst from the cage of my mind. Even the rising dark power within me responded to this tug of new magic, urging me to fly toward it.

But then I felt the desert wind billow up around me and, out of the blue, the bright thread of power I was following suddenly became clear within my murky vision.

It whipped toward me like a rope, taking on a life of its own and burning brightly in the dark. I tried to evade it, but its bright strands looped around my neck even as I angled to the left, a sharp movement.

My survival instincts kicked in and I shifted into my human form, ensuring that my neck was larger before the thread could tighten.

I had a brief thought that if I was lucky, I'd be able to slip the noose by shifting back into my smaller raven form.

Then I crashed into the hot, gritty surface of the dunes and the impact brought my surroundings back to life.

Everything around me was drenched in sunlight once more.

I attempted to grab the thickening magic around my neck, only to become aware of a woman standing mere paces away.

Now, her shadow falls across my face, giving me relief from the glaring sun. I follow the line of her long legs up to the gauzy, white material of her dress scrunched up around her thighs. It barely covers her lower half.

My gaze skims over her hips; catches sight of her

chest; lingers on her neck, where she wears a lace choker; and then moves up to her tilted head. Her hair is the darkest brown and it's billowing around her pale face, brushing her high cheekbones and flying across her brown eyes.

"Who are you?" she murmurs, but it's a quietly spoken question, as if she's trying to figure it out for herself. I guess she doesn't really expect me to respond while the noose is around my neck.

Once again, her voice steals the breath from my chest and I'm acutely aware that I'm completely naked.

I can't seem to control my body's reaction to her presence. It's as if her words are a fucking aphrodisiac, melting away any sensible inhibitions, and my body defies my mental commands not to react.

I'm relieved when she doesn't look below my chest, her focus fixed firmly on my face. I've dropped my satchel somewhere along the way, but with the thread wrapped around my neck and holding me to the ground, I have no chance of retrieving my shorts anytime soon.

The woman drops to my side, releasing her grip on her dress, which bunches between us.

As she leans over me, her loose hair brushes my bare chest, soft and tickling. It takes me a moment to realize she's reaching for the magic around my throat.

She speaks quickly now, although I struggle to make sense of what she says.

"I've never touched a thread of fate. I've never been permitted to go near them. I'm not sure what will happen if I try to release you, but I'm certain what will happen if I don't."

I'll fucking strangle to death.

I try to respond, but it sounds like a snarl.

Even now, I'm conscious of the way the thread is cutting across my hands, making my palms bleed.

"Easy now." She presses one of her palms against the right side of my face, softly cupping my cheek while her other hand cradles my jaw. "I'm sorry if this hurts you."

She sounds genuinely concerned and it confuses me.

She has to be one of the witches I was seeking. Her haunting voice and the power I sense in her touch allows me to identify her as a witch, but she isn't trying to kill me. It doesn't match with the hostility I was expecting to find.

She's so close now that her sweet lips are only inches from mine. My sense of smell is strong and she could be melted chocolate that I want drizzled on the tip of my tongue.

Suddenly, I don't give a fuck about the pain or the thread threatening my life.

Whatever darkness has taken root within me is reacting to her nearness and my only wish is to steal a kiss before I die.

Before I can rear up under her, she slips her hand from my jaw to my neck. I can't see exactly what she does, but the sharp thread transforms beneath my hands. It's far softer and its new texture indicates it's now made of natural fibers.

I'm surprised that it feels like an ordinary rope.

She purses her lips, her head tilted again, a sign of puzzlement. "That's strange," she murmurs. "Glowing fates turned to simple hessian—"

I don't know what she did to force the magical thread to take such an earthly form. All I know for sure is that the rope is loose around my throat. It isn't pulling taut and pinning me to the sand.

I can move.

She seems to realize it at the same instant, her brown eyes clashing with mine.

I surge upward, taking her with me.

Our chests collide and the soft folds of her dress do nothing to stop me from feeling every curve of her body. It only takes me a moment to scoop her legs around my waist, trapping my hard length against her pelvis.

It wasn't a deliberate on my part. I wanted her nearer to me.

But her eyes widen and her lips part with a quickly indrawn breath. Then her eyelids flutter closed. She adjusts the angle of her hips a little, as if she's exploring the sensation.

I haven't spoken a word to her, can't seem to form more than a soft growl in the back of my throat, a satisfied hum.

She's where she should be. In my arms. Taking her pleasure from me.

Her eyes fly open, as if she realized what she was doing. Her hands rest on my shoulders, but she doesn't push against me, her fingertips lightly brushing the muscles across my upper chest.

I'm aware of a structure in the distance that casts shadows at the edge of my vision. It's the same crumbling, sandstone wall I saw earlier, but I don't care to see it better.

Thirst, exhaustion, pain—none of that is important to me right now.

She is all I want. I don't know her name. Don't know if she'll be my end. But I know I need her.

Slowly, she leans closer, her soft, quick breaths whispering across my lips.

Her mouth. I want to explore its curves, taste its contours. I want it crying out with pleasure, moans that resonate in the air and drive every sense out of my head.

I want it wrapped around my—

My head spins, and I don't think it's because of the rush of blood to my already hard body.

I blink rapidly, trying to clear my mind and my vision.

What is this power surging through me? Is it coming from her, or from me?

Whichever it is, it's pulling the ground up toward me.

The strength in my legs crumbles. The rope still resting around my neck hits the back of my left thigh as I drop to my knees and then topple backward.

She wraps her hands around my head, cushioning me from the impact of another fall onto the sand. The heat of the dunes beats through my back as she lands on top of me, her knees on either side of my waist.

I squint up at her, suddenly seeing double.

She's there, dressed in white, her soft curves glowing

against the backdrop of an ever-blue sky and a burning sun—a picture of purity.

But she's also dressed in black, gleaming leather that accentuates her cleavage, her lips forming a sultry curve, and a heat in her eyes that dares me to accept the shadow forming within my own soul.

Her promise echoes around in my mind.

I'll bring you home.

A moment before I black out, my own lips tug into a smile.

I want nothing more.

CHAPTER 5
EMMALINE

T try to catch my breath.

Ripples of sensation flow from every inch where my body is pressed to the shifter's. My inner thighs. My core. My breasts, where I crushed myself against him in my haste to cushion his head from the impact of his fall.

I struggle to categorize the intensity of the pleasure flowing through me. *Is it magic? Darkness? Light?*

It's like being immersed into shadows and finding them treacherously alluring. Warm instead of cold.

My heart is beating fast while my knees dig into the hot sand and my hands are anchored behind the shifter's head.

I try to gather my thoughts, but it's nearly impossible to make sense of the rush of sensations overwhelming me. When he stood up and took me with him, my body had fit perfectly to his, my legs around his waist, my inner thighs pressed to his tanned skin, the friction between our chests sending sharp tingles to my toes.

The heat in my core was even more intense, new sensations that overcame my better judgement.

My cheeks redden to remember how my body had moved of its own accord.

I give myself a hard shake.

He's burning up. Clearly dehydrated and delirious from heat exhaustion.

I'm not sure he even knew what he was doing.

He most definitely needs my help.

Carefully, I pull my hands out from behind his head, wincing when the sand grates against the delicate skin across the backs of my hands. I worry that both my pearl ring and House ring will get bogged in the sand, but I manage to keep them on.

Finally free, I press my palms to the shifter's muscled chest. When I turn my head and rest my ear against his heart, the thudding beat is more rapid than it should be.

I consider his cracked lips, the shadows beneath his eyes, and the dryness of his skin.

The tingle beneath my fingertips tells me there's a magical element to his ailments as well as the physical effects of flying through the desert for what must have been days.

I can't ignore the dark power I sensed when I pushed against the door from my haven. Also disconcerting is the fact that the threads of fate were extending out toward him.

Grimacing, I consider the rope that remains around

his neck, the end of which stretches out for several feet across the sand.

It transformed at my mere touch.

I didn't even try to use magic on it.

For a moment, I consider if there might have been some potion residue on my hands from my potting ventures this morning, but neither belladonna nor sunflowers should have had this effect on the threads of fate.

As quickly as I can, I unravel the side of the rope where it's twisted tightly into a noose, freeing his neck and leaving the rope in the sand.

Whatever's going on here, I don't have any answers, and I certainly don't have any good choices.

If I leave the shifter here, he'll die.

If I take him home, the Crone will kill him. Unless... I can convince her not to. Of the two choices, taking him with me is the only one that might keep him alive.

I know nothing about him, don't know if he deserves to live, but I want to keep him alive for long enough to find out.

My first problem is transporting him across the dunes into our haven. He's tall and broad-chested, and he will weigh more than I can carry.

Unfortunately, levitation is not one of my powers.

I cast my thoughts to the Tree of Lost Things. There could be something among the magical objects that might help me transport him, but that means leaving him here to run back for it.

My shoulders slump a little.

My best course of action is to open a portal back into our haven. Most portal openings require some sort of sacrifice in advance. In my case, I can open small, temporary ones at will, but the sacrifice comes *after*.

I'll be as drained as this shifter currently is, and I'll need to sleep for hours.

When I helped Sky and Zey leave the haven, Sky looked at me with shock when I'd opened a portal for them without any issues. What she didn't see was the aftermath, where I barely made it back to my room to gulp the contents of a nutrient-rich potion—my own special brew—and sleep for an entire day.

The Crone and the Mother didn't think anything of it. They assumed I'd found another lost object and brought it to our home. They're so used to my patterns of behavior that they leave me alone until I emerge from my bedroom again.

I'll need to sleep after I open this portal and during that time, the Crone and the Mother will detect this shifter's presence. It's possible I'll be able to cast a concealment spell on him, just like I can with the objects I find.

I've never tried it on a living being before, but I suppose there's a first time for everything.

Placing my hand over his heart, I draw on the warm power within my chest and allow it to course through my palm as I whisper, "*Protect this raven until I can return him to his loved ones.*"

I don't know who his loved ones might be. His tattoo indicates that he's from the House of Gold and Garnet, and while they're all skilled mercenaries, they're also known for their honor and loyalty to one another.

Of course, what I'm ignoring is that he must be out in this desert for a reason, and as a mercenary, it could be because he was targeting my coven.

He would be foolish to do so. To come after us would be an act of war. We might have an uneasy relationship with Odin and Gabriella, but they would not take kindly to an attack on us. What's more, anyone who came after us wouldn't survive against us for long, no matter how skilled they are.

I repeat the incantation twice, each time more softly, until I sense it take hold of him.

A ripple of power flows over his chest and it makes me gasp. It's far stronger than I was expecting. For a moment, I sense my power combine with another force beneath my palm—a force that's emanating from his heart.

Darkness.

It quickly recedes.

Before I can doubt my actions, I sit upright, draw on my power once more, and wave both hands in a wide arc in the air beside our position.

"*Give me passage to my bedroom,*" I whisper. It's technically not necessary for me to speak my destination aloud for the magic to work, but I don't want to make any mistakes. Heaven forbid, if I accidentally thought of the Crone when I opened the portal and it took me straight to her.

My magic swirls, a sparkling circle in the bright air,

and my bedroom appears on the other side of it. Or, more precisely, my *bed*.

The portal is hovering right beside it. All I have to do is drag the shifter through the opening and onto my bed.

Quickly moving around him, I hook my arms beneath his shoulders, dig in my heels, and drag him around so that his head is pointed in the direction of the opening.

Dear fates, he's heavy. All that muscle.

With another heave, I brace against the sand and pull with all my might.

We slide onto my bed. The shifter's upper body is resting on my legs, and I have to maneuver awkwardly to pull him the rest of the way.

His feet clear the portal and then the opening closes.

I groan with relief and collapse against the cool sheets. I've ended up close to the head of the bed, my back against the pillows and the shifter's head resting on my thigh.

I'm grateful to finally be away from the hot sand. My feet are smarting, and so are my knees from the moments when I knelt in the sand. I may even end up with blisters, although the potion I'm about to drink should stave off anything too awful.

My bed is a four-poster that sits in the middle of my room. The window along the right-hand side looks out to my garden, and vines covered in roses flow through the opening and across the wall on that side.

Potions in vials of lavender-colored glass line the top of the dressing table that sits opposite the bed.

I need to take one of them so I don't get dehydrated

while I'm asleep, but the table feels like it could be a mile away.

Exhaustion is already setting in.

I force myself to move, a fine dusting of sand dropping to the floor, falling from my dress and legs, as I stumble across the rug to the table. I scoop up one of the vials, uncorking it and gulping its contents within seconds. The liquid instantly quenches my thirst, but it won't help with my fatigue.

After quickly grabbing two more vials, I slip open the drawer in my dresser and pull out two long sashes. My hands are shaking now, and I nearly don't make it back to the bed, bumping against the side before I crawl across its surface.

Because of the location of the portal, the shifter is lying neatly in the middle of the bed, his head close to the pillows.

Tying the end of one of the sashes around his wrist, I pull his arm up and tie the other end of the sash around my bedpost. Clambering over him, I do the same with his other arm.

It's not a very effective form of restraint, and he might be able to slip the sashes if he shifts—unless, of course, his arms become his wings and then the restraints might wrap around his feathers.

My only real intention is to slow him down when he wakes up. If I'm still asleep, I don't want him rushing out of my room and getting caught by my sisters.

I collapse against his chest but manage to retrieve the two vials I dropped onto the sheet nearby.

The magical potion will slip down his throat without choking him even if he's unconscious. I designed it that way in case the Mother or the Crone ever needed to administer it to me while I was sleeping.

Lifting the first vial to his mouth, I gently push my finger between his lips and teeth to part them slightly and allow the liquid to flow down his throat. I give him both vials for good measure, given the probable extent of his dehydration.

Finishing my task, I heave a sigh.

I'm determined to pull the sheet around him—since he's still completely naked—and then make my way to the rug on the floor to get my rest, but it seems I've overestimated my remaining energy.

As I attempt to push away from him, the strength in my arms fails and I fall onto his chest. My arms and legs are like jelly, refusing my commands as I slide to his side, my upper leg resting across his stomach and thighs, my chest and dress squished up against his side, and my hair draped across his shoulder.

He smells like hot sand. Bitterly cold nights. The strength of survival.

I should push myself away from him... but I... just can't...

Sleep pulls me down.

CHAPTER 6
SLATER

S hadows dance behind my eyelids, growing stronger with every moment of wakefulness.

I open my gritty eyes just a little, instantly aware of multiple things at once.

My wrists are bound and tied above my head.

I'm naked, but I'm not cold.

Sweet-smelling hair tickles my chin—far too sweet to be so close to me right now.

A warm body lies next to mine. I can't see her face from this angle, but I recognize her chocolate scent and the smooth texture of her linen dress. She's the witch who appeared, like the promise of shelter, in the desert and offered to bring me home.

She's breathing deeply, her upper leg resting heavily across my hip, her arm across my chest, and her palm over my heart as if she's claiming me.

Perhaps it's a good thing my wrists are tied above my head—although I've yet to tip my head back to see what they're tied to. If I were free, I'm not sure I could resist the temptation to follow the sweeping strands of her hair down her back to the delicious curve at her hip, explore the soft skin across the backs of her thighs. Plant kisses against her calves before working my way back up to her hips.

There's a glow around her that intrigues me.

I drag my focus away from her for the quick seconds it takes to assess my surroundings.

A breeze brushes my skin. The sheer curtains at either side of the far window blow gently in the fresh night air.

It's dark outside. Moonlight shines across vines and roses that creep across the wall. Despite my constraints, the bed beneath me is soft, the sheets smooth and silky.

My surroundings hardly constitute a prison cell.

It's certainly not the death I was expecting.

Attempting to wet my lips, I assume I'll find them cracked and my mouth dry, but I'm surprisingly well-hydrated.

I might have been here for an afternoon—or a full cycle through a night and day and back to night. It's hard to tell.

Casting my gaze upward without moving my head too much, I take stock of the silken sashes tied around my arms. It's clear she hasn't had many prisoners before because she didn't finish the knots properly. With a little maneuvering, I'm sure I can easily free myself.

The question is if I should.

I came here for a reason.

Behaving myself is more likely to get me what I want. Even if what I want is rapidly changing.

The witch's hand suddenly trembles where she rests it over my heart. I'm drawn to the wide, lace bracelet that adorns her wrist and the silver chain extending from the base of it down to the ring on her finger.

I startle to see shadows playing around her hand, the glow from the ring keeping them at bay and making them jump and flicker across her fingers, spreading them back over my chest like ghostly ocean waves.

My eyes narrow even further to see scratches across the back of her hand. I vaguely remember her hands cushioning my head. They must have dug into the sand beneath me.

I'm filled with sudden rage at the realization that she's hurt.

Nobody hurts this woman.

Not even me.

A snarl escapes my lips before I can stop it.

She stirs at the sound, stretching against me before settling back into position.

I'm surprised she doesn't immediately jump away from me, but maybe she's too deeply asleep to realize where she's lying.

Not so.

It's clear that she's awake when she tips her head back, a slow but fluid movement, although she has to crane her neck a little to see my face—probably dominated by my chin at this angle.

She's far calmer than I was anticipating and maybe I

should be worried about that. She must be very confident about her power to be so settled about her safety and wellbeing despite my proximity.

"You're alive," she says softly, as if that were her greatest concern. Not the fact that she has a naked stranger in her bed—assuming the bedroom is hers—or that the sound that woke her was my snarl of barely constrained rage.

My anger is slow to dissipate. "You're hurt," I say, a low rumble in the back of my throat.

I barely recognize my own voice and for a moment, worry about the curse sets in again. How far has it progressed now?

Am I still me?

If I'm not… would I even know?

The only clear indication will be the state of my feathers, and I won't be able to extend my wings until she releases me, since I'm lying on my back.

She shoots me a confused glance. "I'm not hurt—"

My glare at the back of her hand directs her attention there.

"Oh," she says. "That's nothing. A few scratches. They'll heal."

Her dismissal halts and her eyes narrow when she lifts her hand from across my heart and the shadows seem to cling to her fingers—defying the jewelry she's wearing —as if they don't want to let her go.

"Well, that's new," she says, but her concern is fleeting.

Once again, she seems more anxious about *my* state

of health. She quickly adjusts her position to slip her upper leg across my stomach and sit up, straddling me.

She continues to surprise me when my nakedness doesn't seem to faze her.

She plants her hands on my chest despite the shadows that gather between us at her touch.

Her hair falls to either side of her face as she stares down at me.

"We don't have much time," she says. "The protection spell I cast on you is wearing off faster than I hoped, and I'm not sure if a second spell will work on you. So tell me: Who are you? And why were you in the desert?"

As she speaks, she runs her flat palms over my chest from my pectoral muscles up to my shoulders, pausing on my tattoo before running up one of my arms, where it's tied above my head.

She has to lean even further forward to reach my forearm and it brings her chest closer to mine. She repeats this with my other arm and it becomes apparent that she's checking me over, her chestnut eyes brimming with concern.

It's difficult to think of anything except the heat growing within me at every brush of her palms, let alone reply to her questions.

She pauses and tries again. "Your tattoo indicates that you belong to the House of Gold and Garnet, is that correct?"

Fuck, it doesn't matter what she's asking me right now.

All I care about is her hands and the intensity of the

sensations they're evoking. Her lips are close to mine, and I fight the urge to surge up off the bed as far as I can and meet her in the middle. My hands may be tied, but there's plenty I can do with my mouth.

Taste her lips. Tear off that choker around her neck—

I jolt because my thoughts went wildly off track.

What the fuck is going on with me?

I'm her prisoner. I'm completely naked. At her mercy. And yet this darkness that has taken root inside me seems to be enjoying my predicament.

"Unbind me and I'll answer all of your questions, darling," I say, again barely recognizing my own voice.

"Hmm." Her expression hardens and disappointment flashes in her eyes. "Not sensible enough to know when to speak plainly."

She removes her palms from my chest, but it's a slow movement when the shadows cling to her hands, and she needs to tug a little. She considers me carefully as she leans back and presses her palms to her thighs.

Her brown eyes take on an even sharper edge and I'm reminded that she's one of *The Three*. Fuck knows what kinds of spells she could cast on me.

The sensible thing to do is to tell her everything. Throw myself on her mercy. The old me would have already explained why I'm here and asked for help.

The fact that I seem unable to articulate any useful responses to her questions... well... It's disconcerting to realize that I'm not in control of my thoughts or impulses anymore.

Thoughts and impulses that are in direct opposition to my survival.

Which might answer the question about whether or not I'm still myself.

It scares the fuck out of me.

But—*damn*—it's impossible to resist the temptation riding my mind as I take in the fall of her hair and her dress. The left-hand side of the white linen is clinging to her curves because of the way she was lying on it, revealing her perfect shape.

"Who are you?" she demands to know.

"I'm—"

My forehead creases when I can't remember.

The euphoria of her touch disappears, and panic starts to creep in, a cold trickle down my spine.

What's my damn name?

"My name is..."

My mind is blank.

Fuck.

I tug on the sash binding my left hand since it feels the loosest. She doesn't miss the action, her lips pursing in worry, but surprisingly, it doesn't appear that she's concerned about me freeing myself.

"You don't remember who you are?" she asks.

I shake my head, a jerky movement.

Her palm lands on my chest again, right over my heart. The shadows leap, but she ignores them. "It's okay," she says, soothing now. "We'll figure it out."

The moment her hand lands on me, my panic eases.

This woman and her touch.

44

I'm not sure if she's healing me or destroying me.

But then I wonder: *Which me? The old or the new?*

My fears grow and my thoughts become more erratic.

All I know for sure right now is that I'm done with these restraints. Pulling my thumbs as close to my palms as I can, I slip my hands free from the silken sashes.

Surging up beneath her, I wrap my arms around her torso and release my wings at the same time. There isn't enough space between the lower edges of my wings and the bed to beat them downward, so instead, I angle them backward. Then push them forward in a strong snap that takes us up into the air. Luckily, her bedroom has a high ceiling.

Her lips part with a quickly indrawn breath and she slips her arms around my back, sliding her hands up the back of my neck and into my hair.

I speak before she does. "Why aren't you afraid of me?"

She shakes her head. "I have no reason to be. You're the one whose life is in danger here."

My gaze lowers to her lips. "You aren't going to kill me. If you were, you could have simply left me in the desert to die."

"The Crone will kill you if you stay much longer," she says with a deadly certainty. "The only question is *when*." Curiosity burns brightly in her eyes. "If you want to live, you need to tell me the truth. Why were you in the desert?"

My response is instinctive. Also accurate. "To find you."

Her head tilts. "Why would you want to find me? Most sensible supernaturals wish to avoid this coven."

"Because you—"

My head suddenly spins. It's the same intense sensation that I experienced when I stood up after the threads of magic pulled me down to the hot sand.

We dip in the air and her arms and legs tighten reflexively around me.

I fight to stay upright, struggling not to pass out. "Because you..." My voice slurs and my words become tangled in my mind. "You... cursed... me..."

No. Wait. That wasn't right.

The furrow in her brow deepens. She appears affronted. "Curses are dark magic. I didn't curse you."

Damn, I'm on the verge of passing out and my only thought is that I can't drop her. I focus as hard as I can on lowering us back to the bed, my wing beats shaky and movements jerky.

I try again. "Cursed... Help... me..."

Not perfect. But better.

I manage to collapse onto the bed without crushing her legs. She's positioned safely on top of me again. I don't have the strength to pull my wings back in. They sprawl beneath me and across each side of the bed, so large that they reach beyond its edges.

"Cursed?" The furrow in her brow clears. Her eyes widen as her focus snaps to the white feathers on my right wing, which flutter at the edge of my vision.

Dancing white spots.

More than three now.

"The feathers on the tree," she whispers. "You lost them."

I exhale heavily. I don't know what she's talking about. Feathers, sure. But why a tree?

I want to ask her what she means, but my voice sticks in my throat, and the dark is pulling me down again.

My feathers are lost.

I'm lost.

CHAPTER 7

EMMALINE

Dark light flickers around my hand as the shifter passes out. He slumps against the pillow, his black hair spread across it, sweat beading on his brow.

Despite his state of unconsciousness, the tension in his muscles remains, making his chest and arms appear even more finely sculpted than when he was awake.

He said he was cursed, and my anxiety now is real.

Curses are dangerous and delicate things. They can worsen at the slightest nudge. Even the smallest wrong move can trigger them. They can take out a single supernatural or obliterate whole buildings or families.

Judging by the dark light that grows stronger when I lean closer, this curse is a powerful one.

I berate myself for not identifying its existence sooner.

Only the darkness of a curse could try to cling to the purity of my magic like these shadows do, both attracting and repelling me. Driven away, and drawn to, my magic.

Entwining with my magic, as if the shadows would consume me the same way that the shifter's dark gaze nearly consumed me.

Even now, I remain on top of him, relishing the sensation of my inner thighs against his hard stomach muscles, inhaling the heat of the desert that seems to cling to him in the cool of the night.

When I woke up next to him, my first thought was not that I should move away, but that I should nestle closer.

My head had fit perfectly to his shoulder, my leg had rested comfortably across him. I'd lifted myself up and straddled him as if I'd done it a thousand times before and it was as natural as breathing.

I wanted to explore the texture of his skin beneath my palms, plant kisses against his chest... slip upward and taste his lips...

"Oh, what a wicked curse," I whisper.

I need to assess its nature as quickly as possible.

More carefully now, I lower my palm toward his chest, assessing the time it takes for the shadows to appear across his heart and rise up toward my palm as if they're reaching up toward me, reacting to my presence.

I make it to an inch above the surface of his chest before they leap upward and touch my hand, a tingling force that strikes through my fingers, along my wrist, up my arm, through my chest, and straight down to my center.

I gasp at the heat that builds between my legs.

Holy—!

Launching myself off him, I barely manage to avoid getting tangled in his wings as I tumble over the side of the bed and onto the floor. I've never been the most athletic person—I've never had to be—and now I land on my butt on the rug, staring up at his wing protruding over the edge of the bed.

My heart pounds and my breathing is rapid as I find my feet. The magic is still riding my body, shadows flickering across my fingertips, and the heat within my core is undeniable.

My thighs clench. My toes curl in the rug.

The shock of pleasure that struck right into my center shivers through me and a soft moan escapes my lips.

I squeeze my eyes shut and give myself a hard shake, finally regaining my sense of equilibrium.

That magic... *damn*... I've never felt anything like it.

I'm standing closest to his right wing now, where the white feathers are ghostly against his ebony plumage. I've already ascertained that the shadows around his body are potent and alive, but now I need to check his wing.

Tugging my dress back into its natural folds and squaring my shoulders, I brace myself as I reach out and hover my palm over the patch of white feathers, slowly drawing nearer to them.

Unlike the shadows, the air around the white feathers is icy. The closer I draw to them, the more I feel the death that has claimed them.

They're lost to him. A symbol of his fading life.

It goes some way to explaining how the black feathers appeared on the Tree of Lost Things.

If I could see the tree right now, I'm sure it would hold five black feathers instead of the three that I saw earlier.

Only a powerful curse could balance itself like this: growing shadows within his body while it carefully steals his life. Keeping him alive while it builds to something.

The question is: What?

I consider what I've observed of him so far...

Slurred speech, dazed eyes, dilated pupils. Memory loss. Repeated bouts of unconsciousness.

At the same time, it's giving him the chance to wake and stay lucid for a stretch of time before it drains him again. But during the time that he was awake, his focus was on me and his gaze seared me.

The way he looked at the scratches on my hand...

It was as if he'd tear down the world to heal them. And yet he couldn't articulate his own need for help.

I give a groan of frustration.

The curse must have been clouding his mind and distracting him with desire.

Only an incredibly complex curse could achieve such a fine balance between its own self-interest—keeping its victim under control—while giving him a sense of power.

I don't need to sense the curse further to understand that it's composed of protective outer layers designed to confuse and misdirect, while the inner layers will be complex magic wound around a powerful core.

I shudder to consider the kind of power that would be

needed to create such a curse, let alone what it is intended to achieve.

Curses always have a purpose. At their most simple, they're intended to cause death or pain—usually as a form of revenge.

But this is no simple curse, and its true purpose is yet to be discovered.

It's possible that the shifter knows the curse's objective, but he's forgotten it, along with his own name.

Keeping my hands away from his white feathers, I gently push on the top of his wing to swing it closed, folding it neatly against his side. A more comfortable position. Rounding the bed, I do the same for his other wing and then I hurry to my closet to find an extra blanket, which I place over his lower extremities.

I bite my lip as I tuck the blanket around his hips and legs, trying to ignore just how perfect his body is and just how closely I was lying next to him.

As I back away from the bed, I sigh heavily into the quiet night.

Whatever dark curse has taken hold of him, it's drawing me closer, triggering sensations I've never had the chance to feel before.

It's *using* me against him.

An emotion I rarely feel rises up within me. *Anger*. I don't usually succumb to it, but the storm of desire in the shifter's eyes gave me a glimpse... just for a moment... of what it would be like to be *wanted*.

I take a moment to exhale the unwelcome anger and focus on what I need to do.

The shifter is dying.

His life is draining before my eyes.

I'm startled to see that another feather is turning white before my eyes—this one on the outside of his wing, where it's clearly visible tucked beside him.

There isn't a potion in my collection that can counteract this curse. My greatest power is my purity, and it's true that I could try to use it to destroy the dark magic growing within him, but this damn curse seems *attracted* to my purity.

It seems to feed off it.

It's too dangerous for me to try to cure the shifter on my own. I could just as easily kill him and fulfill the curse's objective than help him.

On the flip side, the only witches who can assist him are the ones who are most likely to kill him without a second thought: the Mother and the Crone.

As soon as I lift the concealment spell that I've used to hide his presence within our haven, they'll arrive at my door within seconds.

I position myself on the other side of the bed, between the shifter and the closed door, before I return my attention to him.

When I placed the protection spell on him, I'd intended it to last until I could return him to his loved ones, but it's already wearing off.

I mentally seek the threads of the magical web I placed on him. It's difficult to find them with the strength of the curse masking him like a fog. Finally, I locate one of the threads, using my power to tug on it.

It will unravel within seconds and then I need to very quickly surround him with a shield, since I fully expect the Crone and the Mother to storm in here as if we're being attacked.

Tugging on the thread, I whisper, "*Release this raven from your protection so that I might help him.*"

The thread unravels, and golden light streaks briefly across his entire body, glowing beneath the sheets and his visible skin before it disintegrates.

My sisters will be able to detect his presence now, so I need to act quickly, but I also need to keep my cool.

Spinning so that I'm facing the closed door, I calm my mind and draw on the core of my power.

Peace. Heart. Purity.

Each has a place in my power.

The strength of the energy they create always takes me by surprise, the way it rushes through my heart and mind like a tidal wave.

I spread my arms wide and white light bursts around me, spreading from my position to my sides and all the way up to the ceiling before curving in an arc and sealing against the floor on the other side of the bed.

I've created a temporary protective dome around my bed—and the shifter who lies upon it.

Just in time.

The door bursts open and a blast of icy air smashes into me, nearly knocking me to the floor.

CHAPTER 8

EMMALINE

I was ready for the blast of power.

I stand my ground as the freezing air beats against me and a furious whirlwind springs to life in front of me. At the side of the room, my potions smash against the walls. Behind me, the curtains are torn from the windows and fly up to the ceiling, flapping there.

Two figures appear in front of me.

They're both in black dresses, the simple linen ones they wear when they're studying fates. The Mother needs complete darkness to follow the glowing threads of her tapestry, since the weave is so complicated that she can lose the threads if natural light interferes.

Her ebony hair billows around her face, and her emerald eyes are full of fire. Literal fire. It bursts to life in her hands and is reflected across her face as she prepares to use her flames against the intruder.

Beside her, and already a step in front, the Crone's silver hair and bright-blue eyes—the glamour she wears—

perfectly match her icy power. Any logical supernatural would think their two powers would cancel each other out, but no. They work in tandem, freezing and burning in turns, a particularly lethal form of attack that they reserve only for the worst of threats.

They're already lashing out at the shifter on the bed behind me, fire leaping at his head, pouring past me on my left, while sharp icicles shoot toward his legs where they must be visible on my right.

It's only when their magic hits the barrier of my power and shatters against it that they seem to take note of me standing protectively in front of him.

"Emmaline!" the Mother cries, her forehead creased in confusion. "What are you doing?"

"What is the meaning of this?" the Crone demands to know. Her faintly wrinkled, alabaster hands remain outstretched, another wash of her power no doubt only seconds away.

I address the Crone first. "Ethna." Then the Mother. "Eugenia."

I refuse to quail under the weight of their stares or give in under the force of the icy wind beating around me. The whirlwind that brought them here so quickly hasn't abated, although it isn't shrieking quite as loudly now.

"This shifter needs our help."

"Help?" the Crone snaps. "Why would we help a stranger?" Her pale-eyed gaze rakes sharply across him. "And a man, no less."

The Mother has taken a quick step to her right to see

him better and now her expression falls. "Wait, Ethna," she says, speaking urgently. "Don't strike just yet."

The Crone spins to her with an expression of disbelief, but the way the Mother is holding her hands out in front of herself, palms toward the shifter, not attacking, seems to give the Crone pause.

"What is it, Eugenia?" she asks, her voice quieter but no less sharp.

The whirlwind continues to rush around us, plucking at our dresses as the Mother takes a cautious step toward my shield—which I haven't lowered. She won't be able to pass through it, not without suffering severe damage, but its transparency allows her to study the shifter from a distance.

The Mother gasps. "This man's fate has been cut!"

I jolt, remembering the three threads of fate that had reached out toward him and then turned to rope at my touch.

Did I cut his fate?

I shake off that possibility right away. Those threads were striking toward him, not coming *from* him. If his fate has been cut, it must be related to the curse.

"What do you mean?" The Crone lowers her hands and paces toward the edge of my shield. She's so close to me now that her icy power causes goosebumps to form all over my skin. "If his fate were cut, he would have died."

"Undoubtedly, and yet he lives," the Mother replies.

"He's cursed," I say, meeting the Crone's hard eyes. "And it's a powerful one."

"How do you know?" she asks, her eyes narrowed, as if she doubts me.

"He told me—"

"Men lie. They always do," she snaps.

"I sensed the curse for myself." I don't waver. "The many, many layers of it. The most complex curse I've ever encountered."

The Crone draws a sharp breath, as if she's about to dismiss my claim.

My shield will be preventing her from detecting any hint of the curse, but I'm also aware... frighteningly so... that the darkness within the shifter is rising up again.

I feel the hot tendrils of the shadows calling to me, tugging at my back, wanting me to come back so it can connect with my power again. This thick layer of pure magic that I'm maintaining must be very tempting to dark magic that feeds off the light.

Before the Crone can speak, the Mother's soft voice interjects. "If he's cursed, it would explain how he lives even though his fate has been cut. The curse could be creating a bridge between the severed end of his fate and adhering it to someone else's fate, allowing him to live."

"Like a parasite," the Crone says, a low snarl. "All the more reason to kill him."

"But... will his death end the curse?" the Mother asks, edging closer to me. "Or merely cause it to find another host? Or worse, trigger it to complete its purpose—whatever that may be?"

The Crone's shoulders are tense, her lips pinched and brow furrowed, but she finally exhales a frustrated groan. "You're right. We must not kill him until we understand this curse."

She stares down her nose at me. We're the same height, but somehow, she manages to loom over me. "Lower your shield, Emmaline."

I hesitate. "What will you do with him?"

The Crone's expression is cold, and I can only guess what sort of new dungeon she's already constructing within this castle, but the Mother interjects once more. "We need to take him to the tapestry room. Our first step requires locating the severed thread of his fate."

I'm surprised. "Isn't that a dangerous move? To take a cursed being into a place that contains the tapestry?"

"Yes," the Mother says, her simple reply surprising me. "But it's the only way to ensure there is no deception about which thread belongs to him and which other thread his fate might now be clinging to. Once I locate the cut thread, then we can take him somewhere more secure."

The Crone gives a grunt, and it seems she agrees with this plan, even if the pinch of her lips indicates she doesn't like it.

I don't have much choice but to agree.

This is the closest I can currently get to helping him.

Slowly lowering my arms, I call my power back to me. It's a careful process. Normally, I would retract my power with ease, but I'm very aware of the shadows at the edge of my vision and the way they dance and brighten as my power shifts. It feels like any sudden move will cause the dark magic to shoot across the distance and then, I'm not sure how the Crone or the Mother will react to the imminent threat.

As soon as the boundary retracts, the Crone raises her hands and a gust of power rushes across the air, lifting the shifter off the bed. When the blanket falls away, she barely blinks, using her power to manipulate his wings so that they wrap around his body, concealing his naked lower half.

Within moments, he's floating past me toward the door.

The Mother scoops her arm through mine, whisking me after the shifter, and I'm surprised when she gives no indication that she sees the shadows gathering between him and me. "This way, Emmaline."

I allow her to escort me into the corridor. As long as she's taking me in the same direction the Crone is taking the shifter, I have no reason to object to her firm grip on my arm.

We follow the series of corridors that lead to the tapestry room, which is deep within the castle's underground.

The corridors are another illusion. They feel horizontal but actually slope downward, taking us farther down into the depths beneath the castle.

The tapestry room is the darkest space in the whole building and farthest away from natural light.

Finally, we stop in front of the thick, wooden door that guards the room. Like the rest of the castle's rooms and corridors, it's beautiful in its simplicity. It has no markings—nothing that would betray it as leading somewhere important.

The Mother pricks her finger on the single, short needle that protrudes at eye height from the center of the door. At that, the door opens slowly to allow us to enter.

The room is enormous and stretches out into the distance.

It's completely dark, but within it, the tapestry is like a glowing river of threads. It extends from the floor to the ceiling, stretching to the left before it curves, a wide fold so that it can continue snaking side to side throughout the room. There's space to walk down each side and find a point in the past that the Mother might want to examine.

The loose threads on the unfinished edge on the right-hand side are weaving themselves as I watch, the fate of every supernatural who will influence the direction of this world laid bare in front of me.

Well, that is, if I could understand what I was looking at.

It looks like an elaborate cloth to me, made up of many different threads with no discernable pattern.

Only the Mother can truly understand every part of this tapestry.

It's her gift. Also a sort of curse.

We've lived in this world for the past sixty years and there have been times when she has woken us in the night screaming from her nightmares because of things that will come to pass.

Now, she heads straight to the nearest fold on the left, levitating off the ground to study its threads up high, following several of them before lowering herself to the floor.

We give her space, although the Crone is less patient than I am. Once the Crone parks the shifter in the air a safe distance from the tapestry, she begins pacing back and forth, her black dress rustling in the quiet.

The Mother makes an unhappy sound, soft and nearly indiscernible, but my ears prick. I fight the urge to go to her, but the tension in her shoulders and the deep crease of concentration in her brow as she turns to another part of the tapestry tell me to let her think.

I study the floor for a long moment and when I raise my eyes, I'm surprised to find that the shifter has floated closer to me.

At the same time, the Crone has approached the Mother and they both now stand with their backs to me. Neither of them seems to have noticed that the shifter has glided closer to my position.

I feel the tension between him and me like a thread that has wrapped around my heart as surely as the three threads encircled the shifter's neck out in the desert. It pulls me closer to him, and, at the same time, the angle of his body, even in sleep, is practically protective. His wings ruffle a little as if he would extend them.

The number of white feathers have increased. I can see them from the outside of his wings now.

Seven of them.

It's an alarmingly rapid progression from the three he had when he first arrived.

They appear even more ghostly in the darkness of the

tapestry room as the light of the fates flickers across him. His wings are so large that they leave only his head and feet visible. His hair has fallen over his face, unkempt, some grains of sand still clinging to them.

I smother my gasp when he opens his eyes.

Their smoky color seems to meld with the shadows thickening around him.

Behind me, there's a clatter. I swing to see the Mother stumble back from a suddenly glowing thread that extends across the tapestry right in front of her.

The Crone catches her before she can fall, using her power to keep the Mother upright before she reaches her and supports her to regain her footing.

When I turn back to the shifter, his eyes are closed again.

He hasn't moved and the shadows have receded.

I'm sure I didn't imagine it, but there's no indication now that he's awake.

"Emmaline!" the Crone says, her silver hair swinging around her shoulders as she beckons to me. "Come here."

With another glance at the shifter, I hurry across the room.

"What have you found?" I ask, reaching for the Mother's arm.

She's paler than I've ever seen her as she withdraws a fine golden pin that was tucked into the lapel of her bodice.

"Look, but do not touch," she says, using the pin to point at parts of the tapestry.

"This is his thread." She points to a steel-gray strand

that weaves across her tapestry. "His name is Slater Donovan."

Finally, a name. I roll it around on my tongue for a moment. *Slater.*

"What can you tell us about him, Eugenia?" the Crone asks, her voice unusually gentle as she hovers beside the Mother.

When I check the Crone's expression, I find her subdued, possibly even a hint of worry in the tension around her mouth and eyes. I suppose it's not often that the Mother is worried about a fate.

The last time she appeared this way was before the Great Sacrifice.

"I can tell you that his fate before now was interwoven with the fate of Vesperus, the former Gold and Garnet King, as well as with the fate of Kaspian, the new King of that House." The Mother points at two different threads as she speaks, and then to a third thread, a silver one this time.

"That thread there is the fate of the archangel, Nolan," she says. "You will see here, at this point on the thread, they all became entangled with two other fates, both of great power. This one is Nyx, the Goddess of Night, and this darker thread belongs to a witch named Fallon."

She glances back at Slater. "This shifter had loyalty and love in his life. His fate tells me he was honorable in his dealings."

The Mother's pin glides a short distance across the tapestry, showing the interwoven nature of the threads, but then she pauses where the steel-gray thread belonging to the shifter suddenly ends.

"But then, right here, his fate stops," she says.

"And?" the Crone prompts.

The Mother swallows visibly and her hand trembles. "Do you see this transparent section at the end of the thread, which is hiding here?"

The Crone cranes forward, squinting before her eyes widen. "I see it now that you point it out."

"This transparent section makes it look as though the thread were cut, that his fate has ended," the Mother says. "If I were to glance at it, I would assume that this man had lost his life and I wouldn't have given him a second thought."

Upstairs, the Mother was certain that Slater's fate had been cut and that the curse could be adhering the severed end of his fate to someone else's fate.

She continues. "But this transparent section is attempting to mask what his fate is really doing."

I can't remain silent any longer. "Which is?"

"What I feared." The Mother closes her fist around her pin. "His fate has merged with the fate of another."

"Whose?" I ask.

Very slowly, the Mother points her pin at a section of the tapestry just beyond the transparent portion of Slater's fate.

Her chest rises and then she visibly holds her breath as she lightly presses her pin to the tapestry again.

Crack!

A pure-black thread suddenly appears within the

tapestry and sparks up like a bolt of lightning. Power streaks all the way along it to the unwoven edge and explodes into the space beyond.

The air sizzles and the acrid scent of smoke fills the room.

The Mother leaps away from the tapestry, her black dress swishing around her form, the explosion of light nearly sending her sprawling.

I'm frozen where I stand as the wash of power flows across me. It brings with it the heat of fire and the choking thickness of smoke, even though I can't see either of those things.

Nothing in this room appears to have been set alight and the dark light that shot through the tapestry is quickly fading, but the power I feel from it is undeniable.

Somewhere... a battle is raging... and its ferocity turns my blood cold.

The Crone bursts into action, catching the Mother with her power and whisking her backward, scooping me up along the way.

Her power pulls us all to a safe distance.

When she sets me down, I'm shivering despite the strange heat rippling through the air. I find myself drawing closer to Slater while the shadows growing across his body strain toward me as if they want to form a shield around us both.

My instinct is to step close to his side, to feel the brush of his feathers, but a few paces in front of me, the Mother and the Crone are recovering, lifting themselves back to their full height.

They both spin to me.

The Crone's skin shimmers across her face and arms, a sign of her full power building beneath the surface.

Beside her, the Mother's emerald eyes are wide, her form backlit in the final tendrils of power from the explosion.

Her fingers twitch where she grips her tapestry pin, and she speaks in a hoarse whisper. "That thread belongs to a dark creature. One with enough power to destroy all other fates."

CHAPTER 9

EMMALINE

My heart hammers within my chest.

Despite what the Mother said, I draw even closer to Slater.

The Crone is rarely unsettled, but right now, she's paler than I've ever seen her.

"How is this possible?" she asks. "For a dark entity to take over this shifter's fate, it would have had to enter our world first. Surely, we would have felt it. And how does this coincide with his curse? Did the curse allow the dark creature to take control of his mind or is the curse an element of the creature's power?"

Frustration quickly replaces the fear on her face, a deep furrow forming in her brow.

She and the Mother have worked tirelessly to monitor every significant event in our world since the Great Sacrifice. The emergence of a dark power without detection is... well... *Unsettling* doesn't come close.

The Crone takes a deep breath, as if she's trying to cut through her own questions to the most important information. "Could a new entity have crossed through one of the portals without us knowing?" she asks the Mother.

The Mother is shaking her head. "We would have detected it. Just as we sensed Nyx when she came through. And the shapeshifter from Vuulectus."

The Crone is nodding. "And the dark creatures that attacked the phantoms, which led to the creation of the House of Death and Diamond. So then, how did we miss the arrival of this new threat?"

As they continue to debate the situation, I remain close to Slater. Despite their obvious concern, neither of them has told me to move away from him. I guess for now, they are confident enough in their power to restrain or kill him if they have to.

He appears untouched by the explosion, unconscious and unaware of the flurry of fear and worry around him.

When I first saw him out in the desert, much of his true self was still evident in his behavior. He's a raven shifter and he acted like one, using his wings, shifting from his raven form. If a creature is indeed taking over him, then it wasn't completely in control in those moments when he was flying across the sand. It wasn't totally in control in my bedroom, either, because he asked for my help with the curse.

Maybe the curse did allow the creature into his mind, and he was still fighting it at that time. Then, when it took over, he forgot his name and started losing his sense of self.

I suppose that theory makes sense to some degree, but frustration builds within me because the idea of a dark beast controlling this man doesn't sit well with me.

My focus falls to the back of my hand where I scraped myself cushioning his fall. If a creature of darkness had taken over him, he wouldn't have cared about the wounds on my hand.

But he did. His focus was on *me*.

I narrow my eyes at the tapestry, recalling the way the black strand had sparked and exploded with light.

Maybe I imagined it... but... had it curved at the last moment, striking toward me like a thread attempting to complete a loop?

Leaving Slater's side while my sisters remain deep in now-hushed conversation, I approach the tapestry, visually singling out the black thread that has come to rest across the surface of the weave.

I'm not an expert at reading the passage of time in the tapestry, but judging by the distance between the transparent part of the thread and the end of the tapestry where fates are weaving themselves with every passing minute, the first black section of his thread must have happened weeks, if not months, before I saw him in the desert. At that point, his old self should have been dead already and the dark creature completely in control.

But it can't have been, or he wouldn't have come for help.

Again, I return to the fact that he exhibited signs of being in control and knowing his own mind when I first met him.

"What if a new creature hasn't taken over?" I ask quietly, still staring at the thread. "What if it has been Slater all along?"

My question is nearly lost in the constant stream of the Mother's and Crone's hushed discussion, but they fall silent, and I find them both staring at me.

"What did you say?" the Mother asks.

I peer back at Slater as I reply. "You said it looks like a dark creature has taken control of Slater's fate, but what if there isn't a separate entity that somehow crept into our world; what if the curse has triggered part of him to transform?"

I'm gratified when neither of my sisters immediately dismisses the idea.

I point at the tapestry, taking care not to touch it. "This transparent section could be where the curse happened and took hold, and this darkness is his new form emerging."

And gaining power, judging by the way the black thread glitters against the backdrop of the tapestry.

The Mother approaches cautiously, standing close to me as she scrutinizes the tapestry again. She lifts her hand as if she's going to attempt to tug on the thread again but seems to think better of it. "It's possible."

She exchanges a glance with the Crone, who nods and says, "I will need to examine the nature of the curse to discover if it was designed to allow another creature to take over his mind—or if it was designed to trigger a transformation in him."

"Whichever it is, this thread of fate now sits outside the tapestry," the Mother says. "Unless we contain its power, it can only lead to chaos."

"We won't let that happen." The Crone holds her head high and smooths down her dress. "You must stay here, Eugenia," she says to the Mother, "and keep watch over the tapestry. I will take the shifter to a secure place to discover the nature of his curse."

Some of the color returns to the Mother's cheeks now that there is a way forward, but she gives a resolute shake of her head. "The tapestry will be safe enough for now. I worry about what might happen when the shifter wakes up. I'll come with you."

The Crone takes a moment but doesn't argue. "Very well," she says, turning back to Slater once more.

I hurry after her as, with a mere twitch of her fingers, she directs Slater's sleeping form onto his back and propels him toward the door at a smooth glide.

I expect either the Mother or the Crone will tell me to stay where I am, and I'm prepared to fight to go with them, but the Mother beckons me to come with them before she proceeds out into the corridor after the Crone.

Within moments, we've left the tapestry room behind.

When we progress farther into the dark parts of the castle, the Mother flicks her hand, and the lamps light up along the walls, filling them with golden power that casts warm shadows across the walls.

It's a labyrinth down here, and every time I attempt to memorize the passageways, the Crone changes the layout again. I don't think she does it to deliberately disorient me. She simply changes the structure whenever she needs another room for some new purpose.

No sooner has the Mother lit the lamps along the next corridor than a creature moves in the shadows.

A flutter of wings and a loud cawing sound makes us all jump.

I swing to a black bird sitting on top of the lamp directly to my left.

One of its talons is blood-red. Not all of Odin's personal ravens have this feature, but the one he usually sends to us does.

I relax, but the Crone reacts on instinct at its sudden appearance, an indication of how on edge she is right now.

Her icy power hits the wall beside the bird, sending icicles across the stone surface before she seems to recognize the raven. "Oh, for the love of—"

She takes a deep breath, apparently to calm herself, before she strides forward to stand beneath the lamp and glare up at the bird. "I forgot about you," she says, sounding anything but pleased to see the creature.

The bird simply stares down at her, unruffled by how close it came to be being frozen to death.

"Why is one of Odin's ravens here?" I ask, edging

inward and reaching up to coax it off the lamp and onto my arm.

It fluffs its wings before it nestles into my side.

I've never been completely sure how much Odin can see and hear through these birds. Or *feel*, for that matter. But the birds are always willing to cozy up to me if given the chance.

It peers up at me now with its blank, fathomless eyes, as if it knows more secrets than I ever will, but it will never share them with me.

The Crone quickly catches her breath and regains her composure. "Odin sent this raven to update us on the happenings within the House of Fire and Fluorite. At long last, that House has a strong leader who is ensuring the peace is kept." The Crone's lips rise in a self-satisfied smile. "As if we didn't already know."

I can't help my own smile. Twenty-eight years ago, during a time when we more frequently walked this world, a woman came to us and begged us to save her child from its father, a vicious wolf shifter named Mathis Del Reyes. The Crone and the Mother were already concerned about the direction Mathis's fate was taking and agreed to help the woman. We hid the baby within an inconspicuous coven of witches, ensuring her safety all these years.

My smile fades as I remember the events that passed after we hid the baby.

That was when the Great Sacrifice happened.

Blood painted the streets.

Loved ones were lost.

Evil had shown its face.

It nearly destroyed me, trying and almost failing to tip the scales toward the light. A small burst of courage here, a moment of hope there, but the weight of blood and death practically broke me.

After that, we retreated from the world and took refuge in our haven, only emerging when we need to.

For all their hardness, the Crone and the Mother have done everything they can since then to make sure we never see another war between the Houses ever again.

It's why they're so protective of me. If ever such darkness falls over our world, I need to be prepared to fight it.

Now, the Mother sighs. "I suppose in this instance, the raven's presence is useful. We should send it back to Odin immediately and request his presence. Regrettably, our House leaders must be informed of what's happening with this shifter. We've never been particularly friendly with the House of Gold and Garnett, and we don't want to trigger a fight with them."

The Crone's expression twists in the shadow of the corridor. She clearly doesn't like this idea, but it's difficult to argue with the Mother's logic.

I stroke the raven's head as I bend my face to it and whisper the message I want it to convey to Odin, asking him to come to the haven as soon as possible. I add at the end, "And tell him to bring clothing for the shifter, since the shifter has none."

The bird gives a soft squawk before it lifts off my arm and flaps away along the corridor, disappearing into the shadows at the far end. Somehow, those birds never seem to get lost in the labyrinth.

The Crone is already proceeding away from me with Slater firmly controlled by her power, gliding along at her side.

She pulls up sooner than I expected, turning to face a blank stone wall.

"Here," she announces. "I will create a cell to keep him contained."

I grit my teeth at the idea of him being caged, but I can't argue. The Crone needs to do what makes her feel safe and in control of this situation. Caging him is certainly preferable to killing him.

The Crone's power is always like ice, making the hairs on my arms and the back of my neck stand up, no matter how she's using it.

A frosty breeze picks up around my feet and tugs at my dress, lifting my hair and ruffling Slater's feathers when the Crone's power increases.

The Crone clenches both of her fists in front of her mouth, whispering spells over them, before she slowly unfurls her fingers and blows outward.

Her magic gusts forward across the stone wall, which transforms on impact. Stone becomes metal. A room opens up. Bars form at the front. There's nothing inside the cage other than its walls.

The cage door is already open.

She moves Slater inside, changing his position so that he's floating upright near the back of the cell, the soles of his feet only an inch above the floor.

Once we're all inside, the Crone closes the door behind us, locking us inside with him.

"Now to determine the true nature of this curse."

Closing her fists, she brings them to her lips and whispers beneath her breath before she unfurls them and sets her magic free again.

This time, she gives a strong exhale, pushing her palms forward as she cries, "Reveal your curse to me!"

The frosty tendrils of her power wash toward Slater, hitting his wings and wrapping around him in pale-blue bands. As soon as they touch him, they form a glittering pattern of icicles that spread quickly to cover him all the way from his feet up across his feathers and to his neck, their pace slowing when they reach his chin.

That's where they stop, glittering at the edge of his jaw.

At first, I think this was the Crone's intention, but a furrow mars her brow, and she plants her back foot against the floor, straining forward, the muscles in her arms tensing.

Her power billows more strongly, rushing around me and plucking at my dress and hair. A bead of sweat slides down the side of her face. She grunts with effort, pushing her palms forward again, as if she's fighting against a strong opposing force.

Beside me, the Mother takes a step forward, pushing through the force growing within the room. "Ethna?"

The Crone barely acknowledges our sister. Her focus remains on Slater while the blood drains from her already pale face.

"*Curse!*" She forces sound through her clenched teeth. "Reveal yourself to me!"

The icicles on Slater's neck crackle and pop before they can ascend higher than his jaw.

I gasp when his slate-gray eyes shoot open, threaded with glittering onyx, and his wings ruffle around his body.

"No," he snarls.

CHAPTER 10
SLATER

I'*m awake.*

And I feel strong.

Stronger than I've ever felt before.

My mind is sharp, and my thoughts are clear.

I know who I am. I remember my name now. Or at least, I remember who I used to be: Slater Donovan, raven shifter, member of the House of Gold and Garnet.

I also know that I was cursed, but, hell, it doesn't seem like such a problem anymore.

Cursed doesn't seem quite right. *Awakened* feels more accurate.

A new energy has built within my muscles and a buzz ripples through my feathers that urges me to spread my wings and test how fast I can fly. My senses—my ability to see far into the distance and to track and sense magic—were always sharper than most supernaturals', but now they're heightened like sharpened blades.

They allow me to determine the nature of my

surroundings in an instant.

I'm standing in a large cell made of stone walls. The bars at the front of the cage gleam like they consist of mere steel, although I have no doubt they've been infused with magic to ensure that escape won't be easy.

Three witches are poised opposite me, the closest two dressed in black, but it's the third witch, the one dressed in white and standing toward the back, who draws my focus.

The Maiden.

A picture of purity.

The ultimate temptation.

The power now thrumming through me allows me to see behind the shields of purity that have been placed around her and into the core of the power glowing within her chest.

It's fucking breathtaking.

The breath stops in my chest as I take in the strength she harbors inside her—a force she can't possibly know she controls or she wouldn't be standing meekly behind the other two witches.

Her presence makes my heart *thud* and the air I drag into my chest feel alive.

She's the reason I was cursed.

I'm sure of it.

I don't have any logical reason to support that belief, but I know it in my bones.

All of this, I observe in the instant that I open my eyes, and in the next heartbeat, the rest of the room floods in.

The witch closest to me stands with her hands outstretched. She's wearing a glamour that gives the illusion of silver hair, the palest blue eyes, alabaster skin, and a slim figure, but I can see beneath it to her true countenance: crimson eyes, blood-red hair, and black veins that pulse with power.

Right now, she's barely tapping into her full reservoir, but to access it, she'll have to drop the glamour.

She must be the Crone.

Which means the third woman has to be the Mother. She's shorter than the other two. Her skin is light brown and her eyes gleam like emeralds. She wears a bracelet made of three entwined threads that glow against the backdrop of her dress when she presses her hand to her heart. The threads look exactly like the ones that I followed through the desert to find these witches. Exactly like the ones that wound around my neck and dragged me to the sand.

Do the other witches see her bracelet?

The shimmer of a concealment spell around it makes me believe they don't.

While the Crone wears a glamour, and I'm certain the Maiden is unaware of her true power, it seems that the Mother is concealing the fact that she's carrying three entwined fates close to her body. I'm not sure why, and right now, it's the least of my concerns.

The Crone's icy power is wrapped around me like chains, squeezing tightly. It should make me shiver, but I'm warm within the cocoon of my wings.

The rising power within me could break through her

magic instantly and send her sprawling, but I choose to remain still. Only because I don't want to hurt the Maiden.

The Crone's command washes over me. "Reveal yourself to me!"

"No," I say, ruffling my feathers.

She blinks at me, her lips parted, her eyes shooting wide. Clearly startled. I suppose she didn't expect me to wake up, let alone defy her.

Behind her, the Mother and the Maiden have both taken a step forward, their dresses a stark contrast to one another's.

Their expressions are also polar opposites.

The tension around the Mother's mouth and eyes is hard like glass, while the Maiden looks at me with relief, the worried lines across her forehead easing in a way that sends a pang through my dark heart.

"You're awake." Her whisper strikes into me and grabs me like a hook she's wrapping around my chest and using to draw me to her.

At the sound of her voice, the icicles that cover my wings crack apart, shattering quietly and falling to the floor at my feet. I drop the short distance to the cold stone floor as the Crone's power disappears into a fine, white mist.

I'm honestly not sure if the Crone's magic broke because of the power in the Maiden's whisper or because of my body's reaction to her voice. All that matters is that I'm free and ready to fight.

The Crone takes a quick step toward the other

witches, casting alarmed glances between me and the Maiden. "Emmaline! Stay back!"

Emmaline.

My lips curve upward because I finally have the Maiden's name.

She stays right where she is, her gaze colliding with mine, seemingly unafraid of me.

I don't ever want her to be afraid of me.

It's not my intention to hurt her, only protect her. Again, it's pure instinct, but I know with every beat of my heart that this dark shadow within me exists only for her protection.

Emmaline's chest rises as if she's taking a sudden, deep breath. Then she steps forward again, seeming to ignore her sister's warning, hurrying toward me instead of staying away. Her hand is outstretched, palm up, as if she wants to calm me.

"Slater," she says, her voice a wash of power. "Stay calm. We just need to find out what's happened to you."

I act on pure instinct alone.

I need to reach her. Get her the hell out of this cage. Take her far away from here.

Just as I prepare to tuck my wings into my sides and close the unbearable gap between us, the Crone screams. "Stop!"

In the instant before she drops her glamour, I sense her deep fear. She thinks I'm about to cause harm. Hell, I don't blame her. I can't see myself right now, but more dark shadows are gathering at my edges, insidious tendrils rising from my body and reaching out toward the precious woman hurrying toward me. Drawn to the Maiden like I need her to breathe.

Maybe I do.

It must look as if I want to harm her, not wrap her up and shield her from danger.

The Crone retaliates.

She relinquishes her glamour, and her crimson eyes glow like jewels in the cell's dim light. Her inky sleeves fall back as she raises her arms and the black blood running through her veins rises to the surface of her arms, stark against the paleness of her skin.

She whispers rapidly beneath her breath—ancient magic more powerful than should belong in this world. It rivals the darkness inside me, and I'm unprepared for her strength.

Her spell drives me back against the wall with a *thud* that rattles every bone in my body.

It's only because of the strength of the dark power curling around me that she doesn't kill me. My wings fly wide, pressed up against the wall under the force of her attack.

Running toward me, Emmaline screams, "No! Don't kill him—"

The breath whooshes out of her chest when she collides with the Mother's arm. The older witch has stepped into Emmaline's path, hooking her arm around Emmaline's waist and wrenching her to a jolting stop.

"Stop, Emmaline! Don't step into Ethna's power!" the Mother cries, actively pushing Emmaline away from me.

Despite the rush of the Crone's power around my

ears, my sensitive hearing picks up the Mother's voice now also whispering spells. I catch the flash of her emerald eyes glowing with power. I sense the energy surging through her arms and torso as she gives herself the strength she needs to restrain Emmaline and stop her from reaching me.

Emmaline is shouting and struggling to free herself, but the Mother's power wraps around them both, forming a shimmering barrier in the air—against sound and also presumably movement—between Emmaline and me.

I writhe against the wall behind me, the rough stone rasping against my feathers and tearing several free.

Pain strikes through me from the force of the Crone's magic against my chest and the ripping sensation as several more of my feathers tear free. They flutter against the wall at the corner of my vision. They're dull, like old pieces of black paper.

In the next moment, brand new, white feathers sprout and fill the empty spaces on my wings, each fine filament of the new feathers crystalline in its beauty.

The new feathers glow, their light only accentuating the shadows gathered around my body. The darkness is like a growing mist, covering my lower half and clinging to my bare chest.

A new surge of strength rushes through me as I'm reminded of a fundamental truth: Darkness is never so apparent as when it stands against a backdrop of light.

The pain racking my body eases, my eyes narrow, and I strike back.

CHAPTER II
SLATER

S hadows fill the space around me, a dark mist that thickens into the shape of knives. They shoot toward the Crone, their tips glistening as if they've become solid steel.

Her crimson eyes widen, and a shrill cry leaves her lips. She's forced to divert her power from pinning me to the wall so that she can defend herself.

Ancient spells leave her lips, hissed rapidly as she bats her hands back and forth in the air, knocking the knives to the left and right before they can reach her. She hurls them back at me.

I'm not concerned. The shadow knives are of my making. They disintegrate into mist again before reaching me.

In the meantime, the reprieve from the force of her power has allowed me to break free from the wall.

I launch myself toward Emmaline, determined to reach her.

All the while, Emmaline has continued struggling against the Mother's hold. Her chestnut eyes dominate her face as her focus demands that I come for her, her hair swishing wildly around her face.

In the moment before I leap toward her, she shoves at the Mother and, in that heartbeat, shadows play around her fingertips, an explosion of power that finally pushes the Mother out of her way.

Her shadows look the same as mine, appearing to take solid shape beneath her palms like steel plates lending strength to her shove.

I don't have time to wonder why. Maybe I passed some of my shadows on to her during the moments when she slept with me. Maybe it's simply a trick of the light. After all, the dark mist that surrounds me is spilling across this room now and both the Crone and the Mother are struggling to counteract it, their whispered spells becoming more desperate.

All I care about is reaching Emmaline.

Her fingers are stretched out toward me. My hand is reaching toward hers.

Just before our hands would touch, a blast of lightning breaks through the darkness and strikes me in the chest.

The electrical strike knocks me off course so hard that my head spins. I try to use my wing to slow my trajectory into the wall, but I'm moving too fast. All I manage to do is turn so that my right shoulder takes the brunt of the impact instead of my outstretched arm.

I thump into the stone surface, a wash of shadows spreading around me.

Another blast of lightning strikes the wall, only missing my face because I jolt out of the way and drop to a crouch, my wings wrapped tightly at my sides.

A large man strides through the mist toward me, the darkness parting before him. A gaping portal becomes visible in the wall behind him, the opening stretching from the floor to the ceiling. Beyond it, I catch a glimpse of an opulent study with a desk piled high with ancient-looking books and scrolls.

There aren't many gods in this world, and Odin is unmistakable. He's broad-shouldered, a faux fur cloak slung around his body making him look even larger. A black eyepatch sits over one eye while a raven with a red talon perches on one of his shoulders.

The bird doesn't seem the least bit flustered by the lightning sizzling around its master's torso—lightning that has knocked the wind out of me and which I have no doubt Odin won't hesitate to use again if he has to.

"What is the meaning of this?" he roars, his crackling energy cutting through the darkness.

He's now standing between me and the cage door. So are the Crone and the Mother, both of whom have pushed forward. The Crone is surrounded by crimson light while the Mother is glittering emerald. Together with Odin, the two older witches are lighting up this cage like a fucking Christmas tree.

I rapidly assess my options, fighting the overwhelming need to battle my way past them. The odds were already stacked up against me getting past the Mother and the Crone.

I won't survive a clash with Odin as well.

My power is new to me and I'm only controlling it by instinct. I don't even understand what this power *is*. I need more time with it to comprehend how to use it to its full extent.

I take a moment too long to make up my mind and in that time, the Maiden throws herself into the space between me and the others.

White light glows around her and, just like the backdrop of my white feathers, it only makes my shadows appear darker.

Odin pulls up sharply, subduing the lightning that had been rebuilding within his fists, and both the Mother and the Crone halt where they stand.

It's clear that they don't want to hurt her.

Emmaline's presence drives the last of the shadows away, clearing the room as she stands in front of me, her back to me, but I can see that she's holding her arms up, warding the others off.

"Stop," she says. "He isn't our enemy."

"We don't know that yet." The Mother's response is softer than I was expecting, but she's the first to lower her hands, her emerald power fading.

"Let me talk to him," Emmaline responds. "I'm sure he can tell us how he was cursed and why."

She's bluffing. As far as she knows, I can't even remember my own name. But she's doing a damn fine job of sounding convincing, so I don't contradict her.

Odin's shrewd gaze passes across the Maiden and then to me. The press of his lips and the tension around his eyes tells me he doesn't like what he's seeing right now.

Again, I don't blame him.

The Maiden should never put herself in harm's way —not for a raven shifter whose heart has been lost to darkness.

"I recognize this shifter," Odin says. He may only have one eye, but his gaze is piercing. "His name is Slater Donovan. He stands at the left hand of the Gold and Garnet King, Kaspian."

Swinging to the Crone, Odin casts the old witch a sharp glance. The sight of her raw countenance would unsettle anyone, but he seems more concerned about the situation in front of him. "You'd better have a damn good reason for imprisoning him here."

The Crone bristles. "It's why we called you. This shifter invaded our territory and brought a curse with him. We have no choice but to constrain him while we assess the threat he poses to us."

Odin's eyebrows rise before he tips his head in the Mother's direction. His single visible eye narrows, a deeply accusing look. "Mother, you failed to foresee this event in your tapestry of fates?"

The Mother draws herself to her full height, her shoulders stiff. "His fate was cleverly concealed from me. There was no warning."

Odin begins speaking. "So he came here to threaten you—"

The Maiden's clear voice cuts across her leader. "Slater came to ask our help. He knew he was cursed and wanted to be rid of it. He did *not* come here to hurt us."

Odin shifts on the spot and the raven perched on his shoulders ruffles its feathers.

Odin's question is directed at the Crone. "Then why the hell have you not helped him and sent him on his way?"

The Crone whirls to Odin so fast that her black dress swishes around her legs. Despite all the power Odin controls, the god inches away from her.

I guess he's not immune to her raw countenance after all.

"We can't simply wave our hands and cure a curse," the Crone snaps. "We need to understand its nature and purpose first and even then, not all curses can be counteracted. We can't let him go until we know what we're facing."

Odin exhales a heavy breath and folds his arms across his chest. "Well, then, I suppose you'd better get on with it. I will remain here as a witness." He pauses. "In case things go badly."

He casts a softer glance at Emmaline as he follows that up with: "You need to step aside, Maiden."

She's facing away from me, so I can't see her expression, but her shoulders are stiff.

She begins to speak, the tone of her voice indicating a strong protest, but the Mother darts forward, scooping her arm around Emmaline's shoulders. "Hush now, there's nothing more for you to do. You can't help him until we understand this curse."

Emmaline digs in her heels, but I know there's nothing she can do for me, and I need to know about this curse as badly as they do.

"It's okay," I murmur, leaning slightly toward her, withdrawing just as fast when the shadows rise up again between us, dancing at her back.

Despite my soft rumble, she turns immediately.

The worried press of her lips hits me, but I force myself to give her a brief resigned smile. "The sooner we get this over with, the better."

CHAPTER 12

SLATER

At my reassurance, Emmaline finally relaxes beneath the Mother's hold.

She allows the older witch to lead her back toward the cage door, where she stands behind the Crone once again.

Odin reaches for a satchel, which it appears he dropped at the mouth of the portal when he stepped through it. He holds the satchel's handle up to the raven with a softly spoken order. "Take this clothing to Slater. He should be dressed before the curse is examined."

The raven deftly catches the satchel in its talons and flies the bag over to me.

I'm currently crouched, completely naked and without shadows to shroud my lower half now that Emmaline has moved away from me.

I rummage through the bag, withdrawing two pairs of jeans and several shirts, all in different sizes. Choosing the size that should fit me best, I pull on one of the pairs of jeans and then one of the shirts, using my wings for privacy. I'm accustomed to shifting in and out of my raven form and thus experiencing frequent moments of nakedness, but it's a small mercy now to be clothed again.

The two older witches watch me closely, especially when I slip my wing forward to shield myself. I suppose they're worried that I'll do something shady while they can't see.

Then it appears that their attention is drawn to the increasing number of white feathers on my plumage.

I'm conscious of Emmaline's focus more than the others. Her gaze shifts from one feather to the next as if she's counting them, and her lips press into a harder line with each one.

As soon as I open my wings again and drop the satchel to the floor, the Crone moves swiftly.

She whispers a harsh spell beneath her breath, the black blood in her veins pulsing strongly, seconds before I'm wrenched against the cell's back wall.

I don't have time to retract my wings. The impact pushes the air out of my chest, and I can't stop the snarl that rushes between my lips, the only protest I can make.

Once again, my wings are spread wide against the stone surface. I'm back where I started when I woke up. The only difference is that I'm not butt naked.

Odin remains where he is on my left-hand side, his arms folded across his chest, the raven perched on his shoulder. Its head tilts and its black eyes dart between the witches. Odin's expression is inscrutable, but the attention that the raven pays the witches makes me suspect he's using it as another set of eyes within this room so he can watch all of us at once.

The Crone approaches me carefully now. She lowers her arms, but only slightly, the black blood continuing to course visibly through her veins.

The shadows within me recognize how ancient her magic feels, its raw power filled with death and blood.

It makes me wonder how old she is. Witches can live for hundreds of years—and it wouldn't surprise me if the Maiden were much older than she appears to be—but the Crone could be approaching three hundred.

The bloody color of her eyes darkens as her whispers wash over me, spoken in the ancient language.

The dark power within me recognizes what she's saying.

"Cursed one, reveal your corruption."

Corruption?

My indignation rises.

I want to snarl back at her that I may be cursed, but I'm not corrupted, but it's difficult to breathe, let alone speak. The pressure of her power is squeezing my chest so hard, I'm not sure how my ribs haven't broken.

Tendrils of crimson power appear as ribbons, growing from her fingertips and floating toward me. Their edges appear sharp on both sides. So razor-sharp that they gleam in the dim light.

They sail gently toward me, but I have no illusion that they will cut so softly.

Even as my shadows grow around me, attempting to protect me, her power breaches them. The edges of the ribbons slice neatly through the dark mist and continue toward my chest, face, legs, and even my wings.

I tell myself they're made of power, not metal. They won't cut my skin in the traditional sense. Even so, my mind warns me they're going to hurt like hell.

Gritting my teeth, I turn my face away and brace for the pain.

The ribbons sink neatly through the surface of my shirt and jeans without shredding them. Then they're cutting through my skin.

My body goes into shock.

Fuck!

The Crone's power jabs inside my mind and slices through my chest down deep into my internal organs and there's no amount of self-talk that can convince my body it isn't being shredded into tiny pieces right now.

A roar of pain leaves my lips. Sweat breaks out across my face and chest, and the front of my shirt is instantly soaked.

The ribbons of power cut through my thoughts, and I lose all clarity, all sense of who I am and where I am. I'm unable to remain aware of my surroundings. Even the connection with the Maiden is lost, becoming a gaping hole within my heart.

Damn, that hurts the most.

How did she become a part of my soul so quickly?

My roars of pain fill my ears and burning tears streak down my cheeks.

It's the longest fucking minute of my life.

It ends as abruptly as it began. The pain stops and my

eyes flash open to see the crimson ribbons lift away from me and disintegrate into a flurry of red snowflakes. They drop to the floor, forming a carpet at my feet before they disappear.

The Crone has remained opposite me, her arms still raised, her cheeks bloodless. The underlying pressure of her power eases up enough that I can breathe again.

I drag in the air, my chest heaving, while the rest of the room comes into focus.

In the background, Emmaline is struggling to free herself once more. This time, it's Odin who's restraining her, and he doesn't look happy about it. I'm guessing she must have made it past the Mother, and he had to dart forward to keep her back.

The muscles in his biceps bulge and he's holding her close. His red-taloned raven has taken to the air and flaps wildly in the space above his head.

Tears stream down Emmaline's cheeks and she seems unaware that I've stopped roaring with pain.

"Let me go!" she snarls at the god, her voice carrying a harder edge than I've heard in it before.

She manages to free her left arm, and her fist flies out, glancing across Odin's jaw. Shadows splash over his face at the impact, even more darkly visible than when she pushed herself free from the Mother's grasp.

His head jolts back. He grunts and releases her, taking a step back before he tests his jaw. A red patch blossoms across his chin, but it doesn't appear that she broke his bone.

She hunches opposite him, her fist still clenched, her

eyes slowly widening. With a gasp, she unfurls her hand and stares at it, as if she's only now aware of what she did.

Even so, she swings quickly toward me, her tear-stained face turned up to mine.

She's shaking, trembling with rage.

Behind her, the Mother's mouth gapes. "Emmaline!"

Odin waves the older witch away. "I'm fine," he says gruffly. "She didn't harm me."

Emmaline ignores them both, striding toward me. She casts the Crone a stern glance and the oldest witch regards Emmaline cautiously.

Emmaline's chest heaves, fresh tears brimming in her eyes as she contemplates me. I can't see myself to know what she sees, but I'm suddenly aware of the hot tears cooling on my cheeks.

When I swipe at them with the back of my hand, it comes away smeared with blood.

Fuck.

A quick glance tells me that the sweat I thought had soaked my shirt is also blood.

"I hope you got what you wanted," Emmaline snarls at the Crone, her teeth gritted and her cheeks pale. "Because I won't let you touch him again."

CHAPTER 13

EMMALINE

*A*nger.

Twice now, I've felt it, and this time, I can't shake it off so easily.

It's been a long time since I've felt this much heat inside my mind. The kind of fury that clouds my judgement. Not since the Great Sacrifice, when I wept for days because of the death and destruction that was caused and the families that were torn apart. So much senseless loss.

My heart broke over and over.

Even then, my sisters were at my side, providing comfort and reassurance. Ethna and Eugenia gave me a sense of stability and renewed purpose.

Now, my anger is directed *toward* them.

The Crone's lips part in surprise at my declaration that I won't let her touch Slater again.

I dare to turn my back on her, reaching for Slater where he remains pressed against the wall.

Blood is drying against his cheeks where he shed

tears of it. His shirt front is caked with a thin film of blood that must have risen up out of his skin beneath his clothing.

I'm not satisfied with a visual check, gently running my hands over his cheeks, across his shoulders, and carefully lifting his shirt to inspect his skin beneath.

It's smooth and unblemished. The Crone's magic will have drawn out his blood—an extremely painful process —without leaving a cut on him.

My hand returns to his cheek. "I'm sorry," I whisper, wishing I had one of my potions to ease any lingering pain he might be feeling.

He accepts my touch without flinching, his eyelids lowering and his breathing evening out. My hands are tingling where they rest, one on his jaw, the other against his chest, and I'm hyper aware of the strange sensation of magic dancing across my palms where our bodies connect.

His lips part, a whispered exhalation, before he catches my hand in his. A soft touch. "Don't put yourself in danger because of me."

His vocal cords sound lacerated, a consequence, no doubt, of the Crone's ribbons and his subsequent roars of pain.

He retracts his wings, which is a wise move since they can only be a liability in this confined space by making him a larger target.

It's only been seconds since I turned my back on the Crone, but I know I can't extend this moment any longer.

I'd give anything to stay right where I am, but this isn't over.

It's only just begun.

I pivot slowly on the spot, standing with my back to Slater's chest, close enough that he could wrap his arms around me from behind if he chose to.

I can't ignore the fact that I just struck my House leader and knocked the Mother across the cell before that, but I'll deal with the fallout once I'm sure Slater is safe.

"This isn't who we are," I say to the Crone.

She's watching me cautiously, a wary light in her eyes. "Emmaline, I'm sorry you had to witness the shifter's pain, but you know a curse is not an easy thing to assess."

"There are far less painful ways to do it," I snap back.

Her expression hardens. "Not without compromising the findings." She has finally lowered her hands and now she folds them in front of herself. "You were right about this curse."

I'm aware of Slater edging forward so that he's standing to my left, although he remains behind me. My voice is stiff. "In what way?"

"He's undergoing a unique transformation."

Although she's talking about Slater as if he weren't here, she doesn't take her eyes off him.

Behind her, Odin and the Mother draw closer, listening to every word she speaks. Odin's raven settles back down onto his shoulder.

"The shifter's life force is being used like a seed," the

Crone continues. "It's growing into an impossible power."

"What are you saying?" I ask, my tension increasing.

"The curse appears to be harvesting the energy in Slater's life force to grow an immense power source," the Crone replies, calling Slater by his name for once.

Slater is tense and still beside me at the Crone's declaration. What she said makes my blood run cold, driving away the heat of my anger. I was sure Slater was transforming into some sort of new creature, but the Crone wasn't lying about her method of assessing his curse. It's thorough and the results can be trusted.

The Mother speaks up behind the Crone. "Do you mean like a... What did humans once call them?" She thinks for a second. "Like a battery?"

"Exactly like that," the Crone replies. "Energy that can be tapped into to increase a supernatural's power exponentially."

Odin asks the question that has risen to the tip of my tongue. "For what purpose would someone require an energy source like this?"

"I'm afraid it's not possible to know for sure," the Crone replies, which makes Odin's brow furrow. "But when the curse has finished its work, whoever can access the power within Slater's body will be able to accomplish any number of nearly impossible feats."

"Like what?" Odin presses.

The tension around the Crone's eyes grows. "Once the curse has finished its work, I fear there will be enough energy within him to open a new portal. A large one.

Permanent, not merely temporary. The kind an army could march through."

Odin's jaw clenches and his eyes narrow before he casts a barrage of questions at the Crone. "What kind of army? And from where? An existing world or a new one?"

Even though I've never had a strong sense of loyalty or belonging within my House, it's Odin's job to protect the House of Spirit and Sapphire and I have to respect his need for answers. Staying close to Slater, I watch and wait carefully.

The Crone's sharp gaze scrapes past me and rakes over Slater's face. "Judging by the darkness of the power growing within him, it could only be a world of dark magic. The kind of evil that would make Mathis Del Reyes look like a child."

My gaze flickers to Slater. The tension in his shoulders is only increasing. I don't know his history or how he was impacted by the Great Sacrifice, but nearly everyone lost someone they cared about in that war. It looks like he was no exception.

The Crone's focus has shifted to Odin and it gives me a small reprieve from her scrutiny.

Slater is pale. His mind will be foggy after the ribbons. He needs fresh air as soon as possible. I just hope he can hold on long enough for me to convince my sisters to let him out of here.

My hand lifts at my side, a slight movement, but Slater reacts to it, his own hand slowly reaching mine, our fingers touching, and it seems to calm him a little.

Odin blanches at the Crone's mention of evil. "This world would not survive another war between supernaturals. We can't allow that to happen."

"No, we can't," the Crone replies. "Particularly because, if the nature of this shifter's affliction were to become known, any number of powerful witches and warlocks who walk this Earth may try to use his power for their own purposes."

Odin begins to pace, his boots thumping on the floor. "Who could access this power?"

"Certainly the one who created the curse," the Crone replies. "But also any other witch or warlock who understands its nature and chooses to tap into it."

"Including you," Odin points out, his piercing gaze on the Crone.

She stiffens. "Take care not to make unfounded accusations, Odin. Our coven has done nothing but maintain the balance of fates in this world."

Odin stops pacing. "That is true." He gives a heavy exhale. "What solution do you propose?"

"The only way to make sure the curse-maker's purpose does not come to fruition is to find a way to end this curse. And quickly," the Crone says. "Before it can grow in strength."

"How long do we have?" Odin asks.

"Judging by the progressive impact on his feathers, and the building power I sensed, it appears to be progressing rapidly now," the Crone replies. "A week at most. Maybe days before it reaches its peak."

Odin grimaces. "What will happen then? Will the curse kill him?"

The Crone is slower to answer this time. "I have no doubt that the curse-maker will know when the power within him has reached its peak and they will come for him. But the curse itself won't kill him until the energy is harvested."

Her focus flickers back to Slater before she says, "Then he will surely die."

CHAPTER 14
EMMALINE

The soft touch of Slater's fingers becomes a firm grip as he takes my hand into his.

Cold panic has sprung to life within me, making my stomach churn. If what Ethna says is true, then the dark power growing within Slater will become stronger until the curse-maker comes for him. They will take from him the power they created, and that will kill him.

I have no explanation for the connection that has formed between him and me—yet—but I can't simply sit by and watch him die.

"We have to find a way to stop it," I say.

Odin rubs his forehead before he nods in agreement. "For his sake, as much as ours. You must find a way to defeat this curse, destroy the growing power, and return this shifter to his House." His voice hardens. "Whatever it takes."

His focus flashes to the Crone and back to me. "I will

not be the god who allowed war back into this world. I came here to escape the constant battles within my realm. As did you."

The Mother steps forward, speaking quickly. "We won't fail. We've worked too hard to maintain balance within the fates to allow dark magic to tip the scales now."

Odin's stern expression softens. "Indeed, you have, Mother. Is there any way to know who this curse-maker is —or where they are—such that we could deal with them before they can make their move?"

The Mother shakes her head. "I didn't identify any new threads in the tapestry, so it can't be a newcomer to our world. It must be someone who is here already."

The Crone is scratching her chin. "There was no trace of their identity in the curse, either. No magical tether I could follow back to them."

Odin makes an unhappy rumbling sound. "Then that leaves an entire population of suspects."

He rubs his temples, exhaling heavily before he continues. "Ordinarily, I would seek help from other members of my House—they could help track down this curse-maker while you are working on a cure—but I fear that would be unwise. The nature of this magic makes the temptation to use it too great."

He pins the Crone with his steely gaze. "But if you reach a point where you suspect you won't succeed, you must inform me immediately. If that happens, I will need to warn the other House leaders, including Kaspian. He has a right to know what's going on so that he can make decisions about the shifter's fate."

Odin continues before the Crone can reply. "Of course, if you succeed, Slater will return home, whole and well again, and there will have been no harm in keeping this secret."

The Crone has remained standing stiffly. "As Eugenia said, we will not fail. No matter what it takes."

"Good," Odin replies. "Because the fate of this world depends on it. In the meantime, I won't sow the seed of fear among the other Houses."

He rubs his jaw where I thumped him before he gives the Crone and the Mother each a formal nod. "I will leave this in your hands." Pausing, he inclines his head slowly to me. "Be well, Maiden."

He continues toward the wall without a backward glance. Reaching it, he plucks a hair from his beard and presses it to the spot where the temporary opening appeared before.

It looks like a portal, but it's a different kind of magic.

The Crone has designed this lower level of the castle so that portals can't be created to lead in or out of here. My ability to create temporary portals works only in the higher levels and in my garden and beyond.

But years ago, when Odin and Lady Gabriella rose to leadership, the Crone put into place a magical transportation system between our haven and their headquarters in Sydney, Australia.

It can only be triggered by their individual magic. In Odin's case, by sacrificing a hair from his beard.

From this side, it looks like a portal because of the way the wall opens up. Through it, we can see his destination: his study.

Once the opening has spread across the wall, crackling with energy, Odin steps through with the raven perched on his shoulder. The opening closes behind them.

The Crone wears a smile plastered on her face as she turns her attention back to me. "Emmaline, you must prepare healing potions. Slater may need them. While you're doing that, Eugenia and I will consult the ancient texts for a cure. In the meantime, Slater must remain in this cell, where the curse-maker can't reach him."

The Mother was the picture of calm while Odin was present, but now she allows her serene mask to drop. Speaking in a hurry, she says, "Whoever the curse-maker is, they could have followed him here. We need to prepare for an attack."

"Be calm, Eugenia." The Crone presses her palms together. "If they're clever, they'll time their attack for the right moment when they can break in and harvest the magic immediately. I estimate we have at least three days before then. Possibly four. Longer within our walls because of the slowing of time here. I can certainly fortify our defenses before they come near us."

The Crone swings to me. "Now, Emmaline, it's time to—"

"He's not staying in this cell," I say.

The Crone's cheeks flush. "This is the safest place for him. Nobody can get to him in here."

"Neither can sunlight or fresh air," I say, glaring at her. I'm not afraid of her anger.

The Crone opens her mouth—no doubt to retort—but the Mother places her hand on the Crone's arm.

"The shifter isn't our prisoner," she says. "We've assessed the curse now and determined that he can't hurt us." Her gaze flickers over him. "In truth, we are a greater threat to him than he is to us. There is no denying we are all strong enough to harness the magic growing within him and in doing so, we could kill him."

She clears her throat as she takes a step toward Slater, her emerald-green eyes piercing. "I'm sure Slater also understands that we are the only ones with the power to save his life."

"It's why I came here," Slater rasps, his vocal cords continuing to sound tender. "I knew you'd be more likely to kill me than help me, but I was willing to take that chance."

"He could fly out of here if he wants to," the Crone snaps. "Simply shift into his raven form and take to the sky. Then we will have lost the chance to avert the danger that's coming. Are we willing to take that chance?"

"I have more reason to stay than to go," Slater says, squaring his shoulders. "You're my only hope." He shrugs. "Also, the desert will kill me before I reach civilization. I nearly died on the flight here."

The Crone presses her lips together for a charged moment before she exhales. "Very well. You're free to move around within our haven. But be warned that if you try to leave, I will know about it."

She spins to me. "Emmaline, he is your responsibility." Her expression softens a little before she continues. "You must watch out for him and watch *over* him. We must protect him at all costs, even if he is, ultimately, a danger to us."

"I will," I say, a simple promise that places a weight on my shoulders, but it's far lighter than the weight that would have settled over me if I hadn't fought to free Slater from this cage.

I leave his side to scoop up the satchel containing the remaining clothes Odin brought. The brief glance I had of them before indicated that they're all too big for him. And there isn't a pair of boots or other shoes.

I'll try to get the blood out of the clothing he's wearing, since it fits him best, but if I can't, I can try to spin a spell to tighten the larger clothing so the shirt won't billow. Or so the pants won't fall down.

Not that I would mind terribly if they did...

I catch my thoughts, my cheeks heating, before I hold out my hand for Slater. I need him to come with me before the Crone and the Mother change their minds. "This way."

It's a simple gesture, but he hesitates before his hand closes around mine, his palm fitting perfectly to my palm. I realize why he hesitated when my hand tingles and the shimmers building in the air around our entwined hands become visible.

He quickly steps in close beside me, his body—hopefully—blocking the sight of the magic while I tug him forward.

Within moments, we've left the cell behind and I breathe more easily.

When he begins to speak, I place my finger to my lips. I'm sure that my sisters don't have the sort of sensitive hearing that his raven does, but even so, they will be listening.

I take him through the labyrinth of corridors that lead to the first aboveground level on the way to my garden.

"It's okay to speak now," I say.

He doesn't waste a moment. "Where are you taking me?"

"To my garden. I have potions stored there to reduce pain and assist with healing."

"I'm fine," he says gruffly.

I allow myself to smile. "While I'm sure you prefer to wear your scars with pride, the wounds you suffered are internal. I want to be sure they've healed properly."

"You don't need to worry about me—"

I stop walking and swing to him. "As a matter of fact, I do. Even if I didn't care about you personally, the Crone didn't kill you on the spot, and that confirms something very important."

He shifts uneasily but doesn't let go of my hand. "Which is?"

The way his thumb brushes the back of my hand is a distraction as I continue. "Killing you will only free the curse, which would be a very, very bad thing."

He eyes me warily. "Why?"

"This curse must be designed to latch on to the nearest viable host, which would be me or one of my sisters. Imagine the power it could create by feeding from *our* life force. All of which tells me it's vital that I keep you alive."

"Do you think that was the curse-maker's purpose?" he asks. "To use me—a weaker vessel—knowing I would seek you out and likely die on your doorstep, allowing the transfer of the curse to you?"

I can't stop the shudder that shakes me.

He's suddenly galvanized into action, reaching around me and drawing me close. "I won't let anything like that happen."

The breath is snatched from my chest. The corridor around me fades into the background. His firm grip on my hips dominates my senses.

His voice lowers to a rumble that seems to vibrate through me. "I won't let this curse hurt you."

I allow myself to smile. "Then you need to let me look after you."

CHAPTER 15

SLATER

I find myself nodding, consenting to Emmaline's care.

It's not easy for me to agree. I've looked after myself since even before adulthood. Sure, I have a House with a leader and friends who care about me, but it's always been up to me to look out for my health and safety.

One thing she said strikes me above all else: *Even if I didn't care about you personally...*

She cares about me. On a personal level. She said it without any hesitation or guile, as if it were a simple truth.

I stopped second-guessing this impossible connection between us when she stepped between her House members and me.

This connection exists.

The *how* pales in comparison to the unexpected wonder that she makes me feel.

Now, my simple nod seems to be all the agreement she needs.

Her hands slip away from my arms, but she catches my fingers again, a sure grip of my right hand before she resumes leading me along dimly lit corridors.

A whole lot of them.

It's only because of my raven's senses, which are heightened now because of this damn curse, that I keep track of the path Emmaline follows through the maze of corridors and rooms on the way to this garden she spoke of.

Finally, we reach a room with wide-open doors on the other side through which I can see blue sky.

The ceiling and external walls of this room are made of glass. It looks a lot like a greenhouse, except that the air is fresh, not humid. Vines creep across the floor and tall plants grow up against the opposite walls, obscuring the landscape outside.

"Take a deep breath," Emmaline urges me. "Some of the Crone's magic will have lingered in your lungs. The fresh air will help expel it."

I accept her advice and breathe deeply. I'm surprised when I exhale air that is tainted crimson, as if droplets of blood have entered it. My throat suddenly stings like I'm breathing glass shards. The pain nearly stops me from exhaling again, but I force myself to do it.

The breath I expel this time is far less crimson and the pain eases a little, too.

"Keep breathing deeply, even if it hurts," Emmaline

says, the softest command. "Until your breath is clear again."

It takes me ten deep breaths before I exhale a clear breath, and all that time, Emmaline continues to grip my hand. She keeps me walking, as if she understands that movement helps with the pain. Finally, we reach the doorway to the outside, my breathing is easier, and I'm suddenly aware that I'm crushing her hand.

I ease up on my hold and bring her hand to my cheek. "I'm sorry. I didn't mean to hurt you."

I press a kiss to her palm, an apology of sorts that draws a smile to her lips.

"My hand is fine," she says. "How is your throat?"

My brow furrows. "Better."

"And your mind?"

I tip my head with a grimace. "I'm still trying to straighten out my thoughts."

"The sooner you take my potions, the better." She keeps her hand in mine—or maybe it's mine in hers now—as she turns back to the door. "Come into my garden."

Her white dress is bright in the early morning sunlight as she leads me outside.

It's nothing short of an oasis filled with verdant plants. There's a waterfall in a grotto off to my left and a wide patch of lush grass off to my right. Small birds flit from bushes to trees, although it's the single largest tree farther ahead of us that draws the most attention. It seems to have objects attached to it, which is a bit odd.

When I glance back at the building we exited, I'm

surprised to find that it's gone. "Where did the building go?"

Emmaline follows my gaze back the way we came. "The castle is still there. It's hidden within an illusion. It's a protection from the outside world. Just like my garden is hidden from the outside."

I give a quiet grunt. "From the desert, this looks like nothing more than crumbling sandstone."

"The Crone is an expert at magical illusions," she says.

Interesting. "How do you know there aren't other parts of your home you've never seen?" I ask. "Parts that she's hidden from you?"

I expect her to tell me that she has the power to sense them, but she pauses on the path.

"Well, I guess I just have to trust her," she says before urging me back into a quick walk.

Despite the pristine blue sky, a fine mist of water fills the air over the right-hand side of the garden. It looks like a sun shower, except that the rain isn't falling from the sky. I imagine there must be an irrigation system hidden beneath the foliage on the ground.

Emmaline catches me staring at it and gives me a smile as, once again, she seems to read my thoughts. "The plants growing on that side of the garden produce the rain themselves," she says. "Do you see the rainbow they're creating?"

I do. The whole place looks like a fairytale garden. I almost expect to see a unicorn grazing on the wide patch of grass on the right. That would be virtually impossible, of course, because unicorn shifters are all but extinct. Incredibly, I thought I sensed a unicorn shifter in the Fire and Fluorite headquarters when I was there, but I couldn't stick around long enough to find out for sure.

"My potions are this way," Emmaline says, tugging on my hand.

I let her pull me along, reveling in the way her fingertips explore the underside of my wrist as we move. I'm not sure if she's conscious that she's doing it, but I'm not about to tell her to stop.

Her touch is soothing, but it brings home to me the pain that still lingers within my chest, my legs, even the soles of my feet... Other than my throat, which has experienced some reprieve, my whole body aches.

At the same time, I'm trying to process everything I heard in the cell. I have answers to the nature of my curse now, but it isn't good news. Some unknown curse-maker did this to me so they can use me as an energy source—for a purpose that is also unknown, although the possibilities are terrifying.

No matter what the curse-maker's goal is, I'm facing the reality that my life is still on the line. Just like it has been since the curse first touched me.

There aren't many versions of the future where I come out of this alive.

I'm already living on borrowed time. Surviving the desert, being revived by the Maiden, then enduring the Crone's examination. I should have died already.

Odin and the two older witches were in agreement that

nobody can find out about this curse, and I respect their reasons. I understand the threat, and I'll fight with everything I have so that I don't become someone's pawn. Or worse, pass on this curse to Emmaline or her powerful sisters.

But I also have to check in with Kaspian somehow. It's been days since I last gave him an update. I expected to be dead by now. If Kaspian doesn't hear from me soon, he'll send people after me. That could lead to retaliation from the witches or the escalation of an already precarious situation.

I need Emmaline to help me contact him. All I need to do is reassure him that I'm okay and buy myself—and the witches—time.

Resolving to seek Emmaline's help to contact Kaspian, I focus first on getting my strength back.

The path she leads me along is pebbled—some sort of glistening quartz—which is thankfully smooth underfoot since I don't have any shoes.

Emmaline pauses halfway along the path, placing the satchel of clothing onto the ground, before she runs her free hand through the fronds of the flower bushes that reach her waist in height.

"Pain," she mutters as she reaches into the bright-red rose growing on one of the stems and plucks something out of it.

It's a little vial.

When I peer more closely at the other flowers, it becomes apparent that many of them house vials of varying colors.

"Why do you keep your potions here?" I ask, curious about her methods.

Leading me farther along the path, she reaches toward a sunflower and plucks out another tiny vial, this one with golden liquid inside it.

"I discovered that if I store my potions with the plants I use to make them, they keep their potency for far longer," she explains. "Each of them contains living organic material, so maintaining the connection with their origins keeps them alive."

She passes me the red vial first, deftly holding the golden one to her palm with her free fingers. "This one is for the pain."

I'm forced to let go of her hand to remove the cork and lift the vial to my lips. It tastes nothing like it looks. A combination of milk and honey. Its contents flow like nectar down my throat, warming my insides and soothing the residual pain from the Crone's ribbons.

I can't stop my groan of relief, which brings a smile to Emmaline's face.

"Now this one," she says, pressing the golden vial into my palm.

Given how effective the first potion was, I experience no hesitation drinking this one.

It tastes like coconuts and vanilla.

"It's for healing," she says. "I make it from belladonna berries."

I've already swallowed the whole lot, but if I hadn't, I would have spat it out. "Belladonna!" I choke, thumping my chest and forcing myself to breathe. "That's poison."

"Not once I touch it." The corner of her mouth rises into a sweetly crooked smile.

I can't deny that I feel stronger for having taken it. The effects seem slower than the pain relief, but I guess there was more internal damage to repair than I thought.

"Once I touch the belladonna, it transforms into liquid sunflowers and sunshine," she continues. "I was preparing a new batch when I first sensed your presence in the desert."

She shifts on the spot, her focus flickering to the tree in the center of the garden.

"What is it?" I ask softly.

"There's something I want to show you, but I also need to get you cleaned up and into fresh clothing."

I should probably focus on what she wants me to see, but I can't help imagining her washing me herself. "*You're* going to clean me up, huh?"

Color rises to her cheeks, but she doesn't back off. "Of course. I'm not letting you out of my sight."

I hold my tongue. My pride may have fought me on this before, but I've resolved that this woman can take care of me all she wants.

Trying to quell the smile rising to my lips, I say, "There's plenty of time for that." I roll my shoulders to test how much better I feel. "We're here now. You may as well show me what you need me to see."

She scoops up the satchel again. "Follow me."

We head along the path to the large tree I noticed before. It appears to be a willow tree with fronds swooping down all around it and obscuring its trunk.

There are also what appear to be random ribbons, beads, and charms hanging from the ends of its branches that peek through the wash.

My steps slow the closer we get to it.

This is no ordinary tree and the objects hanging from it may look random, but the power glimmering around them is like lightning in my senses.

Each of them calls to me, but it's the saddest sound I've ever heard. Cries of pain and loss.

In the middle of all of them, one spot is brightest, glowing copper within my senses—an object that's hidden behind the outer fall of willow leaves but must be so powerful that it shines through.

Emmaline stops in front of the tree, her head tipped back, a pensive expression settling onto her face as she contemplates each of the objects immediately in front of us.

"These are all unique," I say when she doesn't speak. "They're all powerful. Are they yours?"

She shakes her head, her hair swishing around her shoulders. "This is the Tree of Lost Things. Whenever an object of strong magical power is lost to its owner, I sense it, find it, and bring it to the tree for safekeeping."

"Like you found me," I say.

"Well, that's the thing..." She steps along the path, leading me a bit farther around the tree.

The copper light becomes brighter as I move, as if I'm coming closer to that object, but my attention is drawn to a spot on the outside of the branches.

Fluttering in the morning breeze are ten black feathers.

Emmaline slowly reaches for them, hovering her palm inches away from them.

I sense the heat rising from the feathers. As hot as hell. Their surface begins to sizzle and at the same time, shadows leap up from them.

I lurch forward, catching her around her waist and drawing her back from them, her arm still outstretched, her shoulder pressed to my chest. She tips her head up to see me, her brown eyes scorching me like the heatwaves radiating off the feathers.

She doesn't need to say anything.

"They're mine," I say.

She lowers her arm and wraps it across mine where I hold her waist. "You said that I found you, but..." Her gaze feels like it burns into my soul. "I think *you* found *me*."

CHAPTER 16

EMMALINE

My arm fits neatly over Slater's where he holds me against him.

He pulled me away from the burning heat rising off his lost feathers and hasn't let me go, even though the shimmers of warmth are fading from around the feathers now.

"These feathers appeared on the tree without me retrieving them," I say. "Three arrived on the first day. Now there are ten. That number seems to grow every time a feather on your wing turns white."

Slater's hold is gentle. I could pull out of his arms, but it feels natural to remain where I am. Somehow, now that we're bathed in sunlight and surrounded by the beauty of my garden, the shadows that gather between us don't seem so dark.

They're more like shade.

The kind I'd seek for shelter from the burning sun.

Slater casts his eye around at the other charms on the tree. "All of these things are lost?"

I nod. "I have a knack for finding them. As you can see, there are quite a few."

"You haven't found their owners?"

"There are typically three reasons why," I say, exhaling a soft sigh, "and none of them is good."

"I imagine death is one of those reasons," he says, his voice solemn, at which I nod again.

"What about the other two reasons?" he asks.

"One is if the owner has no emotional attachment to the object. There has to be some sort of emotional connection for me to follow the tether between the object and its former owner."

Slater's forehead creases into quizzical lines. "Why is that a bad thing, exactly?"

"Because each of these objects is powerful. If the owner didn't care about such a powerful object, it speaks to a carelessness that borders on dangerous."

"Fair enough." His focus fixates on a point in the middle of the tree, which is a little confusing because there's no visible object there. "And the third reason?"

This one is harder to explain. I take a moment as I try to put it into words. "The third reason is if the owner is also lost."

The crease returns to his forehead. "Physically lost? Like they don't know where they are? Or do you mean amnesia? Like they've lost their memory, as I nearly did?"

I take another moment before I reply. I have to fight hard not to allow an edge of anger to enter my voice because of the pain that attaches to the objects that have been lost in this way. "I mean if the owner has been forced to abandon their former self."

The crease in his forehead instantly clears. "You mean if something or someone has made them give up who they used to be—and what they used to own."

I'm relieved that he understands, but I can't help but sense a deeper pain in his voice. "Do you have experience of this?"

He exhales heavily. "Before the Great Sacrifice, my family was, well, to put it bluntly, we were filthy rich. My father was a king among raven shifters. I had two older siblings, both ahead of me in line for his position. In the end it didn't matter. They were all killed in the Great Sacrifice. There are raven shifters in other Houses, but my family—my *flock*—is gone."

He gives himself a soft shake but doesn't let me go. "I don't care about the status or the property that I lost. But I know what it's like to have to redefine yourself. To find a new home and a new purpose and leave the past in the past."

"I'm sorry for your loss."

He gazes down at me. "What about you?" he asks. "Do you have family?"

"I have my sisters: the Mother and the Crone."

"I hope you don't mind me asking, but are they your sisters by blood?"

"They're my sisters by fate," I say. "The Great Sacrifice wasn't the first war I experienced. A war was fought in the land of the witches and warlocks where we came from."

His arms tighten around me, as if to comfort me, but I say quickly, "I was a baby. I don't remember any of it. Apparently, it started when a new queen took the throne. The portal between our two worlds had already opened, and witches and warlocks were moving freely between the two worlds, but the new queen was cruel, and many saw their chance to escape by crossing through the portal.

"Of course, she tried to put a stop to it. She killed my family, along with many others. The Crone and the Mother had served the former queen, so they knew some of the secret passageways to reach the portal. They escaped and brought me with them. I'm told it was a difficult journey to get to the portal, let alone past the gatekeepers the queen placed there to stop people from escaping."

"How long ago was this?"

"Sixty years or so," I say.

He's hesitant. "Then, how old are you?"

I give him a smile since I look like I'm in my early twenties. "Oh, sixty years old or so."

"Of course." He doesn't look that surprised. "Witches live long lives."

I grin back at him. "I'm young compared to the Mother and the Crone."

Despite the lightness of my speech, the weight of the past is heavy. I have no remembered connections with the old country. I didn't have the chance to know my parents.

They were killed in an act of cruelty that the Mother

and the Crone refuse to speak about. I know they want to spare me the pain of the details, but there has always been a question mark in my mind. A piece of missing information. An inability to gain complete closure.

"Is that why there's only a small Portal Watch around the portal here in the Sahara?" Slater asks. "The portal that leads into the witch's original world?"

I swallow hard and refocus my thoughts. "They don't have to work hard to keep witches or warlocks from coming into our world because the gatekeepers on the other side do that for them. And it's hard to imagine any witch or warlock wishing to go back to the old country from this side."

Taking a deep breath, I return to the issue at hand, gesturing to the feathers on the tree. "I haven't touched these, but I wondered what might happen if you retrieve them yourself. If it might help slow the curse somehow."

I give him a hopeful look.

When he slips his arms away from around me, I feel colder despite the warmth of the sunlight shining down on the path.

I hold my breath when he approaches the feathers, wondering if they will have the same heated response to his nearness.

My jaw drops a little when, instead of reaching for the feathers, he gently lifts one of the nearby ribbons off the tree.

It's a pale, cornflower-blue color and it belonged to a girl with red hair. She was a wolf shifter who died many years ago. I found the ribbon lost in a garden much like mine—the garden she'd once played in.

The cornflower-blue ribbon contains a binding spell, a simple one that I'm sure was merely intended to keep her hair from flying around her face, but whoever gave it to her wildly misjudged the power in it. Although I don't know how she died, I know the magic in the ribbon didn't hurt her. While powerful, this particular binding spell won't cause harm—unlike some binding spells that are made with dark magic.

What surprises me now is that Slater seems to accurately sense what the ribbon can be used for—particularly when he wraps it carefully around his right hand before positioning himself in front of the clump of lost feathers.

I wasn't sure if they would react the same way around him as they do around me, but heatwaves immediately appear, confirming they are as volatile in his presence as they are in mine.

A look of intense concentration fills his face a moment before his hand swoops upward.

He scoops up the feathers into a bundle, folding the ribbon around them as he pulls them off the tree. They come away easily and the burning-skin scent fades as soon as the ribbon completes its first loop. Whatever volatile magic is growing within these feathers is now bound and subdued.

For a moment, I consider if a binding spell might work on Slater's curse, but the curse has spread throughout his entire body, so binding the curse would mean binding him, too.

I shake off that idea while he quickly ties the material around the feathers so they form a neat bunch.

He gives me a crooked smile as he holds them out to me like an offering of flowers. "My lady."

My lips twitch upward, but any humor he might be trying to draw from me fades since I'm worried about his hand and the burning smell I detected before.

When I reach for his hand, he holds it, palm up, so I can see it. "I'm fine. Not a mark. See?"

I exhale my relief.

He passes me the bundle of feathers before he continues. "Will you to keep these safe for me?"

I hesitate to take them. "You don't want to keep them with you?"

"I think they'll be safer with you."

I take them but continue studying his face. "How did you know the binding magic in this ribbon would subdue the feathers?"

I'm a little ruffled that I didn't think to use the ribbon. Although I try not to use any of the lost objects unless I really need to. They don't belong to me, and my purpose in gathering them is not to amass power. To use these objects without good reason would breach my vow to protect them from misuse.

Slater shrugs, as if it's nothing unusual. "I've always been able to track magic. It's how I found you. But this curse seems to be sending my senses into overdrive." He waves at the other objects on the tree. "They're all calling to me in one way or another."

The black feathers are soft within my hands. "I guess

we'll see if the next feathers you lose join this bunch, or if they come to the tree instead. In the meantime, I'll place a protection spell around this bundle so the power they seem to be accumulating is concealed. The tree protects them, you see, so now I need to place an individual spell on them."

I continue murmuring to myself as I gently hold the bundled feathers and draw on the energy within my heart. "*Protect these feathers until Slater can reclaim them.*"

Repeating the incantation twice, I wait for the spell to take hold before I look up again.

Slater doesn't seem to be paying any attention to my murmurings. He's fixated again on the fronds directly in front of him, even though there aren't any magical objects hanging from them. *Behind them*, yes, but not where they can be seen from the outside.

He said he tracks magic and that all of the objects are calling to him in some way or another, but it shouldn't be possible for him to sense what's within the canopy.

He proves me wrong when he says, "There's something back there."

Reaching forward, he turns his palm to the side so that his fingers slide neatly between the willow fronds.

I startle again, since the protective magic around the tree should stop anyone but me from moving through it. "Wait, you can't—"

He's already disappearing behind the curtain.

CHAPTER 17

EMMALINE

The willow fronds close behind Slater's disappearing form, leaving me gaping. *How did he do that so easily?*

I hurry after him, sensing the brush of magic across my face and arms when I part the leaves.

It's warm and welcoming.

I've nurtured the magic of this tree since the Crone helped me plant the seed from which it grew. It began as a tender sapling that put down strong roots and became the powerful tree that gives shelter to lost things now.

Slater has stopped beneath the canopy, his head tipped back and eyes wide as he peers around the cavern he just stepped into.

There are five caverns like this around the tree. Each one is cordoned off by the wash of willow fronds that fall down from the overhead branches to form walls on either side. The makeshift walls taper inward toward the trunk, creating a triangular shape.

Ahead of us, the tree's trunk glows with soft, cerulean-blue light and so do the branches. The whorls in the tree's bark glow a darker blue while the leaves are lighter, creating glimmers around us.

"Did you create this?" he asks, a low murmur while the ethereal light changes the color of his eyes to glistening stone.

"Yes." I deposit the bundle of feathers inside the entrance and step to his side. "I keep the most powerful objects within these inner caverns. You shouldn't have been able to get past the outer barrier."

He seems to process that for a moment. "I just walked in."

"So you did." My forehead creases. "Maybe it's another side effect of the curse."

"Maybe," he says.

He returns his focus to the copper penny hanging from a chain directly in front of him. The penny has a little hole toward the top through which the chain is threaded. The chain is hooked on a knobby whorl on the branch above his head. "What is this?"

"Ah," I whisper. "That one."

His brow is furrowed. "I sensed its power from outside, but it appears to be a simple penny. I don't detect magic within it—not in the traditional sense—but I'm certain it's powerful." He turns to me. "Am I imagining it?"

"No," I say. "I've protected that coin for twelve years."

"You never found its owner?"

I sigh. "When I'm near the penny, I see only flashes of the woman who owned it." My mind is suddenly far away, overtaken once again by the images that leave my heart hurting. "I see long, blonde hair. The strands are bloodied. I see the curve of her cheek. Also bloody. I hear the clatter when the coin hits the pavement, ripped from the chain around her neck, but the sound is drowned by her scream of pain."

I try to catch my breath, conscious of Slater's hand on my arm, a gesture that brings me back to myself.

Hurriedly, I swipe at the tears burning my eyes. "I found the penny in an alley in No Man's Land. The woman who owned it fought for her life there. She's still alive; I'm sure of it. But she's folded up her old self—her true self—and put herself away in the name of survival. I hope I can find her one day because..."

I swallow hard.

Slater waits quietly for me to continue, but when I don't, he speaks.

"This penny is powerful because of what it embodies," he says.

I nod, pressing my lips together as I try to keep my sadness at bay. "It was given to her by someone who loved her. It carries her memories of being loved. I feel those memories even now. That's why it's powerful."

He reaches for the coin before I can stop him. "Then it shouldn't be left alone."

Deftly slipping the chain from the branch, he reaches for me. "May I?"

I'm finding it difficult to speak. I give him a little nod instead.

Gently brushing my hair to the side, he places the chain around my neck so that the penny nestles at the base of my throat.

"There," he says with a soft smile. "Now you can give it new memories."

The touch of the penny against my skin at the base of my white, lace choker is an intense addition to the emotions I'm already feeling.

Gratitude that he understands the myriad of powers attached to these precious lost things.

Sadness that he has experienced loss himself.

Warmth at his wish to lessen the pain.

And then... beneath it all... the undeniable, slow build of tension within my core.

His fingertips linger at the side of my neck. His thumb brushes my jawline, then the bottom of my earlobe. A light touch.

Since we left the cell, he's been quiet. Far more careful about how he approaches me than when we first met.

But I remember those moments when he wasn't so in control—in the desert and lying on my bed. He pulled me close without any inhibition, and the desire in his eyes sparked the wildest thoughts within my mind.

He's still dressed in his bloodied clothing, although it's well and truly dried now. His hair is tousled and there's a deep shadow of growth across his jaw that's bordering on turning into a beard. The flecks of glittering onyx in his eyes are less bright but only serve to make his irises appear smokier.

I lift my palms to rest them on his chest, simply placing them there as I process this moment between us.

I hope that what I want to ask him won't break it.

I take a calming breath before I speak. "May I kiss you?"

His answering smile chases away any remaining doubts.

His hand wraps behind my neck, cradling the base of my head and sending delicious tingles to my toes. "Fuck, yes."

Carefully rising up on to my tiptoes to reach him, I pause when my lips are a breath away from touching his.

He doesn't swoop down like I thought he might, waiting for me to make the first contact.

His lips are soft, accepting my touch, a contrast with his chest's hard muscles beneath my palms.

His mouth is warm like sunlight. Cool like clouds.

He tastes like flight.

"Raven," I murmur, swaying inward as he pulls me closer.

A slow deepening. His lips move on mine, making my toes scrunch and drawing a moan from me.

The way he cradles my head, the lightness of his touch, only heightens the heat building between us.

Slater's kiss sweeps me away from myself and I may as well be a feather caught in a storm, abandoning myself to the sensations of being carried into darkness, where my thoughts turn wild and my kiss becomes more demanding.

Around me, the cerulean light is tainted by smoky shadows, but they're dancing ribbons, encircling our bodies, twining up and down.

More than anything, I want him to pick me up, scoop my legs around his waist, and press me back against the tree. I'd welcome the hardness of his body between my legs and this time, I wouldn't stop myself from rocking against him, experiencing the pleasure that has been forbidden all my life.

Slater's left hand brushes down my neck, across my lace choker, and his kiss slows. I'm not sure if my choker has reminded him of who I am.

His hands move down my back in slow circles before he plants his palms against my hips, groans against my mouth, and pulls back.

He sways right back toward me as if he regrets breaking the contact and would resume kissing me right away, but again, he stops. His hands tighten on my hips and he closes his eyes briefly as he presses his forehead to mine.

I'm suddenly aware of how rapidly I'm breathing and the way my hands have scrunched in his shirt.

Also, the flicker of his gaze to the shadows gathered around us.

They seem impossibly black against the backdrop of blue light.

"What is this between us?" he asks. "What is this

dark power that springs up every time we touch? Is it my curse?"

I can't suppress my shiver when I see that the shadows gathered across his chest are no longer rippling back from the purity in my pearl ring, but cloaking it in a fine mist, making the gem appear as smoky gray in color as Slater's eyes.

I have no real answers.

All I can do is whisper, "I don't know."

Although I'm certain the Crone and the Mother can't see it.

Slater makes a humming sound. "I thought that might be the case." He refocuses on me where I've remained in his arms, my hands scrunched in his shirt. The shadows gathered across my ring no longer pulse outward across his chest. "Do we have a problem?"

Leaning toward him, I cast aside the caution with which I've lived my whole life. "I'm not sure I care."

Before I can reach his lips, his hands tighten on my hips, halting me.

He softens his action by brushing my jawline. "I think I need to get cleaned up."

CHAPTER 18

SLATER

S topping our kiss was one of the hardest things I've ever done. But I'm not clear on the boundaries that sit between me and Emmaline, and I don't want to hurt her by assuming that she wants to go further —an assumption I have no right to make.

Even if my body hates the fuck out of me right now.

Her hands slowly open, releasing my shirt, and a smile flickers around her mouth.

She doesn't seem perturbed by anything I said, not about the shadows or that I want to get cleaned up.

Striding to the wash of willow fronds that lead outside to her garden, she stoops to pick up the bundle of feathers that she dropped there. Then she turns back and holds out her hand for me. "This way."

I follow, folding my hand over hers as she holds open the willow leaves and we exit the canopy.

I can't help casting a glance back at the magical space I'm leaving behind before the fronds settle back into place. The cavern is a reflection of the beauty of the woman who seems to have captured my heart as easily as she took my hand.

She casts another smile at me, the curve of her lips luminescent.

The sun is ahead of her now, having risen higher in the sky, but its true heat doesn't seem to reach us here. It turns her silhouette golden as she bends again to retrieve the satchel containing the spare clothing and slips the bundled feathers into it.

Then she leads me around the other side of the garden toward the grotto, where water falls into a small pond. Once there, she releases my hand to crouch down to the knee-high plants growing around the edge of the water, whispering to them.

I recognize the cadence of the same ancient language that the Crone spoke when she examined the curse.

Except that the spell Emmaline's speaking has a very different impact.

The greenery around the edge of the grotto rises upward, vines twisting around themselves until they form a circular wall that's taller than I am.

They leave an opening wide enough for one person to walk through.

"After you," Emmaline says, with a gleam in her eye.

I eye the gap in the foliage, not wishing to encounter anything unexpected. Not that I expect something dangerous to leap out at me. Just that this garden has proven unique in many ways already. "Maybe you can go first."

She shrugs. "If you like."

After placing the satchel on the ground, she steps through the opening toward the shallow lip at the edge of the water. The ledge around the pond appears to be just wide enough for one person to stand on it without having to enter the water.

She lifts her skirt to dip her toe into the pond, as if she's testing the temperature, but once again, she whispers ancient words as she moves.

Gentle whisps of steam begin to rise from the pond's surface.

Seeming satisfied with that, she enters the water fully clothed, descending into the pond in increments. The way she steps deeper each time indicates there's some sort of short stairway beneath the surface.

She gives a moan of delight before she immerses herself completely.

I hesitate at the edge of the water, watching for her reappearance.

Moments later, she breaks the surface farther back and stands up on the far side, where the fall of water from the overhead lip of rock is a backdrop to her form. The pond water reaches her waist, running off her head and chest, leaving her dress transparent and clinging to her curves.

"Come in," she says, beckoning to me. "The water's warm now."

Fuck, this woman has enchanted me.

I step onto the ledge at the side of the water, startled

when the wall of vines closes behind me but grateful that it gives us privacy.

I'm not about to step into the pristine water in my dirty clothing, so I draw my bloodied shirt over my head and place it carefully on the ground, where it won't fall in.

Emmaline gives me a smile that stops the breath in my chest before she turns her back on me and lifts her hands to cover her eyes. I take that as my cue to remove my jeans. After which, I step into the water.

No wonder she gave a moan of delight.

This water is instantly soothing to my muscles, drawing away the last of my aches like a poultice draining away bad memories.

I sink beneath the surface, welcoming the calming sensation.

It's impossible to completely forget the curse that's taken hold of me, or the danger ahead of me, but for a few impossible moments as I remain fully immersed, I feel at peace.

The water is so pristine that sunlight stabs through it, and I can see everything beneath the surface. The mossy bottom of the pond slopes upward where Emmaline stands. Her white dress floats around the back of her thighs, caressing her body as she turns in the water.

Needing to take a breath, I emerge reluctantly.

Just as I rise upward, I notice a thin trail of crimson blood that floats from the unruly strands of my hair and cuts across the water.

Damn. Taking my clothing off was not enough. I'm making the water dirty.

I begin to apologize as I find my feet, immersed deeper than Emmaline is. "I shouldn't be washing in this—"

She's already splashing across to me, sinking deeper when she reaches me so that the water's surface laps at the base of her breasts.

"Yes, you should," she says, capturing my arms and drawing me forward until I'm standing at the shallower end.

"Stay there a moment," she says.

I do as I'm told, slightly bemused by her bossiness.

She plucks a lavender-colored object from a patch of purple flowers at the rocky ledge beside the waterfall. When she returns to me, it becomes apparent that it's some sort of spongy substance.

"Be still," she says, running the sponge across my right shoulder and the top of my chest.

It feels mildly abrasive, but not harsh.

I submit to her touch as she sets about cleaning my neck and chest. Even behind my ears. She doesn't go lower than my ribs before she moves around to my back, drawing the sponge across my shoulder blades and all the way down my spine.

I find my eyelids lowering, my body lulled as well as energized.

But thank fuck she's standing behind me because even the now-clouded water isn't opaque enough to conceal what her touch is doing to me.

Her scrubbing slows to languid strokes, and I fight the groan filling my chest. Fight the desire to spin and take her into my arms. Pull her wet body against mine, capture her lips, and explore every soaked inch of her dress where it's pressed to her breasts and thighs.

I catch my breath when she slips her arms around me from behind, the sponge resting against my stomach, her other hand pressed, palm flat, against my heart. The side of her face presses to my back, an unexpected embrace.

"Your heart's pounding," she whispers against my back, the movement of her lips tingling against my skin. "I'm sorry this is happening to you."

She thinks I'm anxious.

I am. There's no doubt about that.

But it's not why my heart is beating hard right now.

I close my eyes. Soak up her touch. Then I turn carefully in her arms, taking care not to knock her off-balance.

My hands find her waist beneath the water, placing a gap between us.

I need this distance, or I'll find myself seeking her consent to do far more than kiss her.

"I'm not sorry I'm here with you," I say, taking a chance to express what I'm thinking.

She tips her head back, the sunlight catching the deep-brown hues of her eyes and her wet hair. The light glints off the penny I placed around her neck, reminding me of the way her voice hardened when she spoke about it. Her quiet rage resonated within my sensitive hearing like the thump of drums.

Now, her breathing increases and her focus shifts to my lips. "I'm not sorry to be here with you, either."

Her left hand finds my right bicep, her touch energizing me as her palm glides all the way up to my shoulder. As she moves, the gap diminishes between us until her chest is a mere inch away from pressing against mine.

She reaches up, lifting herself a little, probably on tiptoes, although I can't see her feet through the water to tell for sure.

"I felt something," she whispers, her eyes searching mine, "in that first moment when we met in the desert and you hauled me into your arms."

I remember every second of it.

"It was indefinably dark and overwhelmingly enticing," she continues, speaking slowly and carefully. "I can't begin to understand it, but I need to feel it again. I *want* to feel it again."

My hands tighten on her hips for the second it takes me to engage my muscles and respond to her request.

I pull her up against me, scooping her legs around my waist, and, this time, deliberately trapping my hard length against her pelvis.

Water rushes off her. Her breasts press against my chest, her hands clasped around the back of my neck. The tightened nubs of her nipples make me groan when they rub against my skin as she draws herself high enough to reach my lips and kiss me.

She moans against my mouth as she tightens her legs around me, her core pressed to mine.

Her eyes close. So do mine as she rocks against me,

and I tell myself she can explore this sensation as long as she damn well likes. No matter how much the shadows draw and tighten around us. I ignore them because once again, I'm filled with the certainty that she is where she should be.

Her chest rises and falls rapidly where she's pressed against me, but a crease mars her forehead as she draws back. Her fingertips play in my hair as she searches my eyes. "How do I ask for more?"

"Just like that," I rumble.

The water churns around us as I turn and carry her to the back of the grotto. I'm sure I saw a lip of rock behind the waterfall where I might be able to sit her down.

When I carry her through the thin downpour, I'm gratified to find a shallow cave behind it.

The cave looks high enough to stand up in and wide enough to lie down in. The walls seem to be made of sandstone, although it has an unusual grain. When my palms brush against the rocky edge, I'm surprised to find that it's soft and gives a little. Not hard like the stone I expected.

The water laps at the edge of the rock at my waist height. It's the perfect height to set her down and explore her body while the waterfall forms a shimmering barrier at our backs between us and the rest of the pond.

Her backside slaps softly against the surface as I place her down, her dress hitched up to her thighs and pooling at her sides.

Running my hands up her back, I capture her mouth again, tasting her sweetness, drinking the droplets of water that have gathered around her lips, exploring the perfect curves of her mouth.

Fuck, I could become lost just by kissing her.

I barely break the contact between us even when I leave her lips to nudge and kiss her chin, working my way across her jaw to her neck, flicking her earlobe with my tongue in the same way that I intend to tease her breasts.

When I reach them.

Which could be a while since I don't intend to miss an inch of this woman's body.

Her breathing is rapid already, but I want it moaning from her lips before I reach her most sensitive places.

Her hands tighten against my back, gripping me hard as she whispers into my ear. "I want to betray my vow."

I work my way back to her lips, drawing out the sensation of her tongue on mine before I force myself to focus on what she said. "Your vow?"

She exhales a breathy moan. "I'm the Maiden."

My mind is clouded by desire, intent only on drawing out every second of her pleasure, but her simple response is like cold water slapping across my face. "The Maiden."

Fuck. Of course.

I draw back a little, trying to refocus my thoughts while her arms remain around me, keeping me close.

"We live by the harmony of three," she murmurs as she closes the small gap between us to plant slow kisses across my jaw. "The Maiden, the Mother, and the Crone."

The path of her lips continues across to the corner of my mouth. "My coven is not like others. We have defined, traditional roles from which we draw power. The Crone is vengeful. The Mother is wise. And I..." She pulls away a little, takes a deep breath, and then exhales it. "I am pure."

I draw my conclusions and speak them bluntly, not because I want to embarrass her, but because I don't want to misunderstand the boundaries of her consent. "You're not supposed to have sex."

She gives a slight nod. "That's correct."

Her fingertips continue to play across my back as I think it through. Given what we've already been doing, I say, "But you're allowed to kiss me."

It's a question more than a statement, since I'm not sure of the extent to which she's already broken the rules by which she's supposed to live her life.

"I'm allowed to kiss you," she confirms.

I nudge her lips again since that isn't forbidden. Then I divert to the side of her neck, brushing soft kisses to her skin. "What about here?"

Her eyes close and she leans into me. "You can kiss me there."

"Hmm." I hum against her neck and delight in the way she shivers beneath my touch.

Dipping my head lower, reaching the top of her shoulder, I ask, "And here?"

"There is fine, too."

I work my way around the curve of her shoulder while my other hand brushes her neck and jaw.

Then I dare to proceed lower, hovering above her breast. My gaze rises to hers, a questioning glance, before

I blow gently across the wet material clinging to her pert nipple.

She gasps. Moans.

I want nothing more than to make her moan again, but I rein in my response and fight to maintain my control as I ask, "What about here?"

CHAPTER 19

EMMALINE

I'm lost in the desire riding my body.

Slater's touch consumes my senses, so much that I barely notice the ribbons of darkness lingering around us and connecting us.

I never imagined I could feel so much need that I would be tempted to break my vow and destroy my purpose.

His shadowed gaze holds mine as he hovers, seconds away from delivering the pleasure he's promising me but holding back until I give my consent.

Heat fills my heart and mind. "Everywhere," I gasp. "Everywhere is fine."

His jaw clenches. His hands continue to stroke my neck, my shoulders, but still, he holds back.

"But no sex?" he asks, pushing me for more. "Tell me what that means, Emmaline. Where is the boundary?"

Every time he speaks, his breath puffs across my breast and the wet material of my dress is like a conductor of sensations, making my head spin with pleasure.

I attempt to form sensible speech, fighting the burn within my cheeks as a touch of inhibition returns to me. "You can't enter me."

He takes a moment, appearing to give this thought, but then the tension in his shoulders fades and his lips curve upward a little. A smile that drives a dark thrill through me.

"So I can touch you everywhere with my mouth and hands," he summarizes, "but I can't fuck you in the traditional sense."

"That's correct," I whisper, wishing I could say *yes* to all of it.

His smile grows as his hand strokes down to my stomach. "What about with my fingers?"

Now it's my turn to take a moment. While his thumb strokes back and forth across the gathered folds of my dress, I consider the rules of my life.

I must remain pure, but where is the exact line?

Maybe it's a matter of choice in this case, a decision over which I have *some* agency.

My lips part with a heated breath. "Fingers are fine."

His dark gaze flashes at me before he lowers his head to my chest and takes my nipple into his mouth, his tongue flicking over it through the material of my dress. At my moan, he deepens the pressure while his hand finds my other breast, playing across the hard nub hiding beneath my dress.

Pleasure burns through me, only building the longer

that he touches me. The heat between my legs demands release. The wetness now growing there has nothing to do with the pond we bathed in.

He slips his hands beneath the bunched-up hem of my dress to take hold of my underpants, urging me to lean back so I can lift my hips.

He frees me of my underpants but takes every opportunity to explore my legs at the same time, focusing on my right leg, which he hooks across his shoulder as he kisses, nuzzles, and tastes his way up to my inner thigh.

I gasp, moan when he finally reaches my core. He parts the folds, his fingertips gliding along the sensitive edges before his mouth closes over me, his tongue swirling across my clit.

I'm still sitting, my right leg hooked across his shoulder, and I plant my hands against the soft sandstone on either side of me as my head tips back.

The intensity of my desire hits me hard—harder when he slips a single finger inside me, a careful and shallow push, sliding in and out before moving deeper. All while his tongue swirls against my aching center.

I'm moaning and tipping my hips by instinct to give him better access. Whispering for more. "Give me more."

I sense him smile against me before he fills me with two fingers, deep inside, and then I'm lost to the rhythm.

I close my eyes and take it all. Every overwhelming, aching second of it until my senses burst and my mind fills with pleasure that makes me want to scream.

Sweet fates.

Returning to myself, I exhale slowly into the humid

air, my breath blowing through the shadows that have gathered like mist around us.

My heart is pounding. My breathing is rapid.

Slater looks up and gives me a lazy smile a moment before he surges up out of the water, his wings appearing for the beat it takes him to wrap his arms around my waist and lift me to my feet.

His wings retract just as soon as he lifts me a step inside the cave, where he places me down. His arms remain around me while he plants kisses on my lips and chin, making a satisfied humming sound in his throat.

"There," he says, as if my orgasm is all he needs.

It sparks a new desire within me.

All of my inhibitions have vanished.

"Let me touch you," I say.

One corner of his mouth hitches up. "I can take care of my own needs soon enough."

I bite my lip, dampening the urge to run my palms down his body and take his hard length into my hands. Or possibly into my mouth...

As if he reads my thoughts and intends to dissuade me, he places me to the side. Now that he's no longer pressed against me, it allows my dress to fall around my legs, covering my body again.

My dress hides the wash of my wetness that slides down the insides of my thighs when gravity takes hold. It might have embarrassed me before, but I welcome it as a reminder of every intoxicating moment of pleasure he gave me.

He strokes the hair back from my face. "Just give me a minute. I'll be out soon."

"If you're sure," I say as I step back from him and, with a daring look at him, slip my dress up over my head.

It slaps against the stone when I drop it to the ground, leaving me naked now except for my jewelry.

His hungry gaze travels from my face to my feet, lingering on my curves, pausing on my thighs, where I'm sure my wetness glistens between my legs.

When his focus rises to my face again, I give him a challenging smile.

"I'll leave you then," I say. "Assuming you don't change your mind before I go."

I pause for a moment before turning toward the lip of rock, preparing to slip back into the pond and splash my way through the waterfall.

He catches my hand before I can move away.

Pulling me back to him, he lifts me so that his mouth can crash against mine.

"Show me how," I say, pulling back just enough to speak, my lips moving against his.

My hand is already traveling to his stomach.

I want to hold him, want to know the feel of him against my palm.

With a groan, he urges me to the side of the cave so that my back is to the grotto wall. The soft surface hugs my shoulder blades and backside when he presses me to it.

His voice is thick with desire as he lowers his lips to my mouth. "Will you trust me not to break your vow?"

I give him a nod without hesitation.

He's already proven I can trust him.

His hands run down my sides to my hips. "Close your legs."

I do as he asks.

He presses forward, one hand on his cock, guiding it between my legs.

The tip rubs against my clit before he adjusts his angle downward, until he's snugly captured between my wet thighs.

He pulls back a little before pushing forward again.

His groan joins my own moan of pleasure as the top side of his length slides against my clit with each slow in and out.

My thighs clench around him, an instinctive response, as my wetness increases, aided by gravity. It eases his quickening movements.

His grip on my hips tightens before he responds to my next moan by lifting his right hand to cup my breast, then arching down to take my nipple into his mouth.

My moan turns into a cry.

He asked me to trust him. But I'm not sure I can trust *myself* right now. He's so close to me and all I want is for him to bury his cock inside me and ease the aching need rising once again within me.

With all my willpower, I keep my legs tightly clamped and resist the urge to reach down and guide him inside me, to take every hard thrust as he finally seems to abandon his control, driving himself against my thighs. Driving me to frantic heights of need.

He raises his head from my breast and his lips capture mine, his tongue demanding access to my mouth while he buries himself between my legs one last time with a deep groan.

He jerks, shudders, and his hands hit the wall on either side of me.

But while his orgasm seems to have been complete, my own body is screaming at me with a desire I don't think I can ease without him.

He doesn't seem to miss a second of my response. His hands capture my face, one palm on each cheek. "Emmaline?"

I'm gasping. Panting. Rocking against him with unbridled need. Only to find that he's hardening again and it's like a trigger that causes me to push forward, my hand reaching for him, determined to draw him inside me and sate this overwhelming desire.

His eyes widen, a heated beat where he catches his breath, his gaze raking across my face and my parted lips.

I haven't come anywhere close to taking hold of him before he pushes me back against the wall, a move I almost fight. His hands are firm on my hips as he drops to his knees in front of me.

He buries his head between my legs, his tongue working my clit in savage strokes.

I groan with relief as he feeds the dark desire building within me with every rough grind of his tongue, the hard press of his left hand against my hips, and the thrust of his fingers within my body.

His possessive growls vibrate against me, and they push me over the edge.

I tip my head back, not caring when I knock myself against the sandstone, and throw my hand over my mouth to smother my scream as the orgasm breaks across me.

The release is complete and my legs are left boneless. I slide down into Slater's arms and he draws me to the cave floor. I'm wrapped up in him and wrapped around him, my head nestled against his shoulder.

Our breathing is ragged and takes long minutes to settle, our bodies slowly relaxing against the stone. I created this grotto myself and it took me many years to succeed in making the stone soft and cushiony. It's my private space. A place to curl up and sleep in if I want. I never dreamed I would welcome its softness as much as I do right now.

Slater strokes my back in long, sweeping motions that calm me, even though the press of my naked body against his reminds me of what he can give me.

Finally easing my head back to see him, I whisper, "Is this fate?"

"I want to believe it is." His voice is low and soft as he continues stroking my back. "Otherwise, I have no explanation for this connection between us."

A question rises to my lips that makes me feel vulnerable, but I ask it anyway. "Are we fated mates?"

Slater thinks on this for a moment before he replies. "My former king found his fated mate. But he said that he knew she was his mate as soon as he saw her. When I first saw you..." He grimaces. "I was half out of my mind. Deep in darkness."

"Oh." My heart sinks a little. I was drawn to Slater. I wanted to help him. But I didn't have a sudden moment of clarity where I knew he was my mate. "Then I guess we can't be."

I'm surprised when he challenges me. "Why not?"

My eyes widen. "But you just said..."

"You pulled me from the darkness," he says vehemently. "Your touch kept me alive. Maybe this curse destroyed the chance for our souls to recognize each other from the first moment we saw each other. But I won't let that diminish the chance to spend my final days with you."

His final days.

I'm suddenly stricken. "You don't think you're going to survive this, do you?"

He doesn't answer me. He presses his lips to my cheek, kissing away the tears that have sprung to life and are trickling down my face.

"I don't know what's going to happen," he says finally. "But I don't give a fuck if we can't call each other 'fated mates' in the usual sense. This curse brought me to you, and the connection I feel with you is undeniable."

A swell of sadness fills my throat and it's impossible to speak. I've never come so close to breaking my vow. I've never opened myself up to any kind of intimate touch, let alone opened my heart to the possibility that I could have a mate.

Now, within a short timeframe, Slater has cracked apart walls I spent years building around myself.

I don't fully understand how.

Maybe it *is* fate. A mating that was destined and inevitable but clouded by the magic of a dark curse.

All I know for sure is that he's woken a need inside of me that I've kept at bay for years.

Not just a physical need, but an emotional one, because for the first time, I've chosen to make my heart vulnerable to being hurt and now there's no going back.

CHAPTER 20
SLATER

Emmaline falls asleep in my arms.

It takes me a long time to get my thoughts and my body under control. She triggers desires in me that I know are unattainable, but that doesn't stop me from wanting them.

The purely physical wants will be easy enough to deal with, but the emotional ones are scraping at my heart.

I don't remember much about my father, but I do remember that he never considered showing emotion to be a weakness. Ravens, by nature, are intuitive, and he expected us to express our thoughts. That might have been one reason why I fit well into the House of Gold and Garnet. The former king, Vesperus, wasn't afraid to acknowledge his feelings and neither is Kaspian.

But now, my emotions feel like my enemy.

If I listened to them—if I gave in to my most basic instincts—I'd gather Emmaline up and fly her away from here right now. It's the same instinct I felt when I woke up in the cage and she was hurrying toward me. I wanted to reach her and get her out of that cage. Get her out of this place.

I have no rational basis for that impulse, and it's baffling in its intensity.

I shake myself a little too hard and she stirs in my arms, opening her luminous, chestnut eyes. Her lips are blushed with color, bruised a little from my kisses, and her cheeks are glowing.

She stretches against me with a sigh. Then a light crease forms in her forehead. "I fell asleep."

I stroke back her hair. "We should get cleaned up."

She breaks into a grin. "That sounds like a good idea."

We take our time finding our feet and by the time we step back through the waterfall, I've left new kisses on her lips and fought the desire to taste her all over again.

I'm surprised to find the pond's water pristine again. No hint of the blood that washed off me earlier.

Emmaline explains that the magic within the water makes it self-cleaning, and she adds that it won't cause the skin to look like prunes—which would explain why I stood for so long in it and didn't notice any effects.

We immerse ourselves, still naked, and take our time to wash.

I'm concerned that the Mother and the Crone will come looking for Emmaline, but she assures me that they're unlikely to emerge from their books until dinnertime.

"Maybe not even then," she says. "Once they have a purpose, they're single-minded until they achieve it. They'll only come looking for me if they find a cure for the curse."

"What about the defenses that the Crone wanted to place around your home?"

"She can cast those spells from a distance. She doesn't need to come down here for that." Emmaline swills her hand through the water. Her gaze becomes distant for a moment before she refocuses on me. "In fact, she already has."

Water slides down her arm as she lifts it. "There are extra barriers across the sky and all around the outer walls now." She pins me with a suddenly worried look. "All the more reason for you to avoid flying, in case you trigger a defense."

It's a good thing I didn't give in to my impulses earlier, then.

"Do they often leave you alone?" I ask, curious.

"Often," she says, tipping her head back into the water and rinsing her hair.

I'm accustomed to living in a busy House, being sent out on missions, and working in a team more often than I work alone. As I consider the wall of vines around the grotto and cast my mind to the stone wall around Emmaline's garden, I murmur, "Your life is bordered by walls."

When she lifts herself from the water again, glistening droplets fall down her bare chest, following her curves. "But none of us is truly free."

The water swills around her as she closes the gap between us.

She runs her fingertips across my chest, following the shape of my tattoo—the sign of my fealty to my House.

"We all live within borders," she says before she steps away from me, squeezing the water from her hair as she steps out of the pond.

She reaches the top step, and the vines open at her approach. When she pauses in the gap, she tips her head back, her eyes closed as she accepts the sun's rays on her face.

It must be midday by now, but it's difficult to tell since the sun's rays are filtered here.

It's difficult for me to reconcile the serenity that Emmaline is exhibiting now with the fierce need she revealed to me inside the cave.

Then she casts a glance back at me, her lips slightly parted, her lashes lowered a little, and I glimpse again the *wild* in her nature that she must be keeping tightly constrained.

My body's response to her is instant, but I don't try to hide it, since it brings a glorious flush to her cheeks when she sees it.

Still naked, she stalks out of view, returning a moment later with the satchel in hand. She's also holding a clean linen dress, which she pulls over her head after placing the satchel down.

I don't miss the fact that she hasn't bothered with underpants.

"How did you procure new clothing so fast?" I ask,

curious about her methods and trying to distract myself from the temptation of her body.

"A witch has her ways." She gives me a mysterious smile before she capitulates and explains. "I often bathe in this grotto. I've set up the vines to give me privacy, and I keep a stash of dresses in a little box right here."

She opens the satchel and withdraws a pair of jeans, underpants, and a T-shirt—all of which are easily two sizes too large for me. The bloodied clothing has remained on the ledge where I first took it off, and she ignores it, seeming to favor the fresh clothing.

She scrunches the new items in her arms and, with a whispered spell, the material visibly shrinks in her hands, becoming a smaller bundle.

I step out from the pond, shaking off as much of the water as I can before I take the offered clothing.

"Wait," she says before I attempt to pull it over my still-wet body. "Stand in the opening, close your eyes, and look up at the sun. It will dry you."

So that's what she was doing when she paused in the opening.

She steps back into her garden, which gives me space to maneuver, and I do as she instructed, welcoming the evaporation of the water from my chest and legs. It's much easier to dress now.

"The clothing fits me perfectly," I say.

She gives me a smile. "I had the chance to explore your body and figure out your size. Let me know if you need anything else, and I'll do my best to help you."

Behind me, the vines slowly lower back to the ground

and now I can see the small box she spoke of before. It's green, as if it's made entirely of plant matter, and nestled into the bushes around it.

A weight settles on my shoulders as reality returns to me with every step I take away from the grotto.

"Actually, there is something I need."

She spins back to me. "Tell me."

I hesitate, but there's no easy way to ask. "I need to contact my king. If he doesn't hear from me soon, he'll send people to look for me."

She purses her lips, her forehead creased, and I'm surprised when she doesn't immediately say *no*.

"Kaspian Antonik is an honorable king," she says. "If he knows what's really going on, he will want to help you." She's shaking her head. "If you speak with him, you can't tell him about the nature of the curse."

"It's in my best interests to keep that to myself," I say. "Kaspian wouldn't harm me, but I don't want to be hunted by others for the power they think they can get from me."

"But how to accomplish this?" Emmaline mutters, as if to herself. "You won't get past Ethna's defenses if you try to leave this haven. And we don't keep any sort of communications technology here. We only have direct contact with our House leaders, and that's strictly through ravens or in person so our messages can't be intercepted or interpreted by anyone else."

She raises her eyes to mine. "It also helps us to stay under the radar, since the streams of magic that are used in telephones and other communication devices can be traced."

I wait patiently while she chews her lip, seeming deep in thought.

"But maybe I could open a portal directly to your leader," she says. "You could speak with him face to face as long as you don't step through to the other side."

She searches my face intently as she speaks, and I understand her wariness. She trusted me with her body, but now she'll have to trust that I won't take my chance to leave.

"If I leave, I'll die," I say quietly. "And in the worst way possible, given that my death could unleash some sort of hell on this world. My only hope is to stay."

"Okay, then," she says. "I'll need energy for this. A meal first. And it's best if I open the portal from within my room so I can sleep easily afterward."

"Sleep?"

She gives me a wan smile. "Opening portals drains me. I need to sleep for hours afterward."

I'm quiet. "Then you're also trusting me to stay with you after you fall asleep."

She chews her lip. "I won't be able to watch over you. Which is why I need you to remember that Ethna will retaliate if you try to leave."

I maintain her gaze. "I know you only have my word for it, but I'll stay with you. Watch over you while you sleep."

She gives me a quick nod before she leads me back along the path.

If I didn't already know that a castle lies ahead of us, I'd think we were headed toward a forest of trees. Another illusion at the back of her garden.

At the last possible moment, the forest vanishes, becoming the vine-covered glass walls of the atrium at the front of what I can now see is a colossal building.

When I exited the glass atrium earlier this morning, the castle had already vanished by the time I looked back, but now I have the chance to follow the soaring lines up into the sky. It hits me just how vast this palace is.

Incredibly large for three witches.

Of course, that may be one of its defenses. By forming a maze, an invader could become lost within it.

"The kitchen is this way," Emmaline says, leading me across the atrium and through another labyrinth of corridors.

The farther we walk, the more I notice a pattern to our path and the changes in the air around us. What strikes me most is that the air is always fresh, even when there are no visible windows or doors.

I stop halfway along the next corridor. "How much of this is an illusion?"

Emmaline gives me a grin. "A lot of it. It's designed to look more complex than it is. But unless you know how to read the magic within these walls, you won't find your way without me."

She points to the doorway at the end of the hall. "We're here."

Inside, the kitchen is homely and simple. Most electrical items that humans once used are now powered by magic, although they've retained their general shape and structure.

A wide-open window at the side of the room lets in sunlight and fresh air, revealing a view of the garden we left behind. Its proximity to the outside seems to be more evidence that the castle is set out in a way that's intended to feel as if I've walked farther than I actually have.

Emmaline tells me to take a seat at the little, wooden table, but I offer to help cut the bread she retrieves from the bread box, along with the fruit she places in front of me, while she busies herself cooking eggs.

She hums while she works and the whole room seems calmer for it.

I find myself breathing more deeply than I have for days. Relaxing more than I have for...

Damn.

It's been years since I felt this sort of warmth.

This sort of peace.

For a few moments as we work side by side, I catch a glimpse of a future I may never have. This beautiful, wild, ethereal woman standing at my side while we do mundane things. Prepare food. Set out plates.

The harmony I feel right now is at odds with the knowledge that darkness is growing within me. Yet I feel calm about it.

I can't even seem to muster surprise when I realize that the shadows that swirl between us have become so constant that they blend nearly completely into our surroundings. They've become a mere hint of dark light that I can only discern if I look for them.

Emmaline doesn't seem to be looking for them, either, paying no heed to the little flares of power as she moves through the beams of sunlight from the table to the stove.

Finally, she gestures for me to sit down as she dishes out the eggs onto the crusty bread.

I eat slowly, but she consumes her meal with gusto.

"Dear fates, I was famished." She groans.

Swallowing her final mouthful, she reaches for a piece of fruit—a berry that appears a lot like a strawberry except that it's a deep shade of purple.

Instead of popping it into her mouth, she holds it out for me. "These are lavender-berries. I cultivated them myself. Try one."

She looks at me with anticipation, and I suspect I'm the first outsider to partake of this particular kind of berry.

I lean forward, taking the fruit into my mouth along with the tip of her finger, sucking on both.

She catches her breath, and I keep on sucking. Capturing her hand, I chase the juice down to her palm, exploring the delicate creases with my tongue. Her other hand flutters against the table and I resist the temptation to lift it, follow the edges of her lace bracelet with my tongue all the way down to her pearl ring.

Her eyes close and a moan sighs through her lips— lips that I capture in mine, closing the gap between us within seconds and pulling her up into my arms. I place her on the table a moment later and wrap her legs around my hips.

There's berry juice on my lips and she devours it, her

tongue darting out to taste my skin.

I can't kiss her enough.

Her forehead, her cheeks, her jaw. Her breasts through the fresh linen covering her torso.

My hands find the base of her dress where it's hitched up across her thighs and my palms slip to her lower back and upward, reveling in the way she arches into my touch.

Her bare skin is heated, her breathing rapid.

She said we can't be fated mates, but I refuse to dismiss the possibility because I have no other explanation for this intense need I feel for her.

I want nothing more than to claim her, call her mate, and vow to protect her for as long as we live.

Except that could be a very short time for me.

If my days are numbered, then I'm grateful to spend them with her. But I also fear that I should try to shake off this certainty I feel about her, put aside the possibility that she is the one for me, because...

What does it mean for her if I die?

"Slater?" She reaches for my face, her palm sticky with berry juice, and I'm tempted to suck on her fingers all over again.

"Hmm?"

She plants a soft kiss on my lips. "Where did you go just now?"

"Somewhere dark."

She brushes her fingertip against my jaw. Her legs tighten around my hips. She speaks softly. Vehemently. "I won't let this curse take you."

CHAPTER 21

EMMALINE

Despite my promise to Slater, I've never felt so powerless.

I'm trusting the Crone and the Mother to find a cure for his curse. In the meantime, I'll watch over him in case the curse-maker comes for him, but I can't help but feel there must be more I could be doing.

I promise myself that, once Slater contacts his king, I'll find a way to consult the spellbooks myself and help in the search for a cure.

Right now, I want nothing more than to explore his body all over again, but I promised him a conversation with his leader.

Planting a kiss on the underside of his jaw, I say, "You need to contact your king. We should go to my bedroom now."

His eyes flare with heat. "Yes, we should."

I can't stop my smile. "Not for that. To open a portal."

"Of course." He returns my smile, brushing a final

kiss across my palm before he steps back to allow me to slip off the table.

"The biggest challenge we face is discovering where Kaspian might be," I say as I retrieve the satchel once again and lead Slater along the path of corridors toward my bedroom. "It will be dangerous to open a portal somewhere out in the open or to open it where others might overhear our conversation."

Slater doesn't seem worried.

"That shouldn't be a problem," he says. "Kaspian won't go far from his manor right now."

"Oh?"

Slater is unusually closed off. "He has a reason to stay close to home."

His response piques my curiosity, but if he's not willing to elaborate, then I decide I should respect that.

I'm aware of his laser-sharp focus as he takes in everything about his surroundings. Even though I told him he would need my help to get around the castle, I have no doubt that he'll figure out the navigation system soon enough.

He refocuses on me. "Can you open a portal to a place you've never seen?"

"I can, as long as I'm able to verbalize clear directions. I'll need you to describe the manor for me and where Kaspian is most likely to be."

Slater gives me a description of the Gold and Garnet headquarters in Reykjavik, Iceland. It's the exact opposite of my home here in the Sahara—icy cold, although

Slater describes the sky as being as crisp blue, as it is above this haven.

"If you direct the portal to open to the heart of the manor, it should take you to Kaspian's personal quarters," Slater suggests.

"Okay, then." I'm feeling prepared until I open my bedroom door, and then the disarray hits me.

"Oh, no." With a sinking stomach, I remember how the potions sitting on top of the dressing table were smashed in the whirlwind the Crone created when she literally blew into my room last night.

Slater reacts to the tension in my voice, instantly on edge as he sweeps into my room. "What's wrong?"

Even as he speaks, he's heading to the far side of the room, quickly checking the window and then the adjoining bathroom. He moves like a soldier clearing a room, and I'm reminded that he's a trained mercenary.

He pauses at the window, his shoulders suddenly tense, but my focus is on the smashed glass on my dressing table.

"My potions," I say, placing the satchel inside the doorway and hurrying to the table. Dropping to my knees, I check the floor on the far side in case any of the vials have remained intact.

A glint of purple catches my eye and I'm relieved to spy a single lavender-colored vial lying against the wall.

Thank the fates.

Retrieving the vial, I rise back to my feet, preparing to tell Slater it's all fine because I found a vial after all, but he's already reaching for me.

His hand closes around my arm, a firm grip. His voice is vehement—the same vehemence with which I declared that I wouldn't let the curse take him.

"I've been stupid and selfish," he says. "I can't let you put yourself in harm's way like this."

"I'll be fine," I say. "I have a potion."

I hold it up for him to see, but his jaw remains clenched. "That's not what I'm talking about."

The muscles in his jaw are so tight that I consider him carefully. "Then... what is it? You know I trust you not to leave while I'm sleeping."

"But that only takes into account the threat to me, not the threat to you."

"What threat...?"

"The curse-maker," he says. "You'll be vulnerable while you're sleeping if they get through the Crone's defenses. I won't put you in danger like that."

Before I can speak—remind him that the curse-maker is unlikely to turn up for days—he continues. "I'll find another way to contact Kaspian."

My jaw drops a little because the intensely protective look he's giving me is one I would normally associate with wolf shifters protecting their mates.

Perhaps ravens have similar instincts. I haven't met enough of them to know for sure.

My hand closes over his. "I won't be in danger," I say quietly, lifting my eyes to his. "Because you'll be watching over me."

His expression softens, but he doesn't relent. "Your

sisters made it clear I'm not strong enough to fight the curse-maker."

Again, I want to remind him that the curse-maker won't be here for days and even then, they'll have to fight their way past the Crone's magic, but I stop myself because there's more going on with him.

He's acting on pure instinct right now, and I can't ignore the possibility that his intuition is warning him about some danger that I can't yet sense. After all, he told me that his senses are heightened right now.

"Do you think my sisters are right?" I ask quietly. "That you wouldn't be able to fight the curse-maker?" My hand tightens over his. "Slater, you stood beside King Vesperus and now King Kaspian. You're a member of the House of Gold and Garnet, renowned for its skilled mercenaries. You wouldn't have survived all these years without the ability to win a fight, no matter the power of your opponent."

I step in close to him, feeling the sudden icy heat of the darkness within him responding to the command in my voice. "You will protect me, Slater. I trust you."

He stares down at me, the friction between us increasing before he swoops down and his mouth clashes with mine in a kiss that snatches the breath from my chest.

When he pulls back, my heart hurts a little at the worry in his eyes, but there's determination too. "Where do you want to do this?"

"Right beside my bed," I say. "That way, I can fall onto it if I collapse without warning."

I remove the lid from the vial and drink the potion in one swift go. I'm instantly energized, which is just as well because this portal opening will be more difficult than most—and not only because I'll have to search carefully for Kaspian.

"Before I open the portal, I'm going to place a protection spell around us," I say. "It will conceal the portal opening from my sisters. They're accustomed to me creating portals to retrieve lost items and won't normally think anything of it, but they'll be alert to any sort of portal opening today."

Slater gives a soft grunt. "They'll think I'm trying to leave." But he follows that up with: "Will it protect you while you sleep?"

I shake my head. "I'm afraid not. It will only remain intact while I'm awake. Opening the portal at the same time as maintaining the protection spell will drain me more quickly, so I won't be able to keep the portal open for long."

"I understand," he says. "I'll speak with Kaspian as quickly as I can."

When I position myself on the edge of the bed, Slater takes a seat beside me.

To draw on the core of my power, I calm my mind and focus on the combined forces of peace, heart, and purity that exist within me.

White light bursts from my body faster than ever, arching up as high as the ceiling and as wide as the walls, forming the shape of a dome that reaches all the way to the other side of the bed behind us and across to my window in front of us.

I'm pleased that it will completely enclose the portal, but now comes the hard part.

I stand, knowing I need to choose my speech carefully.

Drawing on my power again, I extend both hands in a wide arc. *"Give me passage to the heart of Kaspian's manor."*

I hold my breath as my magic creates a growing circle in the air at the side of my bed.

As the opening expands, a large room comes into view.

So far, so good, but then...

A figure moves on the far side of the room.

A woman stands at the window.

She spins toward the portal. Her blonde-brown hair swishes around her curvy silhouette, which is backlit by soft sunlight. Through the window, I glimpse the crisp, blue sky above a harbor—most likely Reykjavik Harbour —so I can't be far off my target.

I immediately recognize her as another witch, and the nature of her power makes my heart sink.

This woman controls death magic.

CHAPTER 22
EMMALINE

Death magic is the antithesis of my own power. We can't expose the nature of Slater's curse to anyone else, let alone a witch who controls such dark magic.

At the same time that fear builds within me, I'm confused about why the portal opened to her and not to Kaspian. I asked for the heart of his—

Oh.

His heart.

He must care for this woman and that's why the portal brought me here. It's only because of the possibility that she might be an ally and not a foe that I don't snap the portal closed immediately.

The witch's vibrant-green eyes are wide with surprise as she stares at the portal—and then through it. "Slater?"

She seems to recognize Slater at the same moment that he recognizes her.

"Fallon?"

"What is this?" she asks, hurrying toward the portal before she pulls up sharply, her hand raised as if she's sensing the nature of the magic that has invaded her space and is wary of it.

The portal crackles around the edges, a sharper sizzle than usual as I fight to keep it open and retain the protection shield at the same time.

Slater shoots me a worried glance before he takes a swift look at Fallon's surroundings. "Is Kaspian with you?"

"Not right now." She studies the portal warily and eyes me with as much caution. Even across the distance, I can sense the potently dark nature of her power. "I think he's in the next room."

Damn. I can't help but berate myself for allowing an emotional element to enter my portal directions, but it seems that my own heart is influencing my actions right now.

Fallon pins Slater with a firm look. "What's going on?"

"I need to speak with Kaspian urgently," he replies, without explaining anything.

Her brow furrows and her lips press with apparent frustration, but then she folds her arms across her chest and lifts her head high. "Well, I'd call him in here, but I don't exactly control my jailer."

Jailer?

I flash Slater a questioning glance, but he's focused on Fallon.

"Can you give him a message for me?" Slater asks her. "It's important and we don't have much time."

Her eyebrows rise. "Being a glorified prisoner isn't enough? I have to be a messenger now, too?"

Any shred of concern I have that she's being mistreated vanishes at her retort. Whatever's going on between this witch and Kaspian, Fallon seems to be holding her own. I recall Slater's cryptic comment about Kaspian having a reason to stay close to home right now. If I weren't so worried about Slater—and about the intensity of the power tingling through my body—I might even admire Fallon's pluck.

Slater grimaces at her response. "Will you tell him that I'm okay? It's important that he trusts me to contact him when the time is right. I don't want him sending anyone after me. Can you tell him that?"

"I can," she says. "When he graces me with his presence."

The tension in Slater's shoulders eases. "Thank you, Fallon."

I also breathe a sigh of relief, preparing to close off the portal.

"Wait!" Fallon's quick gaze flashes from my choker down to my ring. She addresses me directly this time. "You're the Maiden."

"I am," I reply.

Her brow is furrowed and as she peers through the portal, the glow in her cheeks fades. I sense the spark of her power as her attention shifts back to Slater. "You're shrouded in death."

Of course, her power will detect the curse.

We're on dangerous ground now, but Slater seems intent on alleviating her concerns. I understand why, since we want her to deliver a message to Kaspian that ensures he doesn't act out of concern for Slater's wellbeing.

"I'll be fine," he says. "Tell Kaspian—"

"Not you, Slater," she says, swinging back to me. "*You*, Maiden."

"Me?" My eyes widen. I try to catch my breath as a cold sensation creeps down my spine and knots form in my stomach.

Her expression softens. "I'm not a Seer, and I don't know the future, but death is all around you." Her focus flashes back to Slater. "*Between* you. And it's only growing stronger."

Slater begins to speak again, this time with a warning tone in his voice.

"Fallon, I'm fine. I need Kaspian to know I'm fine or he'll send people after me. If you mention death—"

"He'll overreact and put you in chains," she deadpans, making my eyebrows inch upward a little. "Or, I'm sorry. I mean, he'll put you in a suite and make you his personal prisoner."

"Fallon—"

She waves him off. "I get it, Slater. I'll tell him your message and leave the rest alone. I wouldn't want to give King Alphahole another reason to question my magic."

The portal crackles again, sparking at the edges of my vision, and I shudder at how volatile it seems to be. Slater has delivered his message and I don't want to keep the portal open longer than necessary.

Dropping my hands, I close it off. The magic swooshes inward, snapping to a bright spot that fades slowly. The glowing light overhead that forms the protective dome also peels back and vanishes, leaving the room darker than before.

My arms drop to my sides.

I anticipate the exhaustion that's bound to overwhelm me now.

"Fuck, I hope I didn't make things worse," Slater says, rubbing his temples.

"I believe she'll do her best to deliver the message without stirring things up." I scoot up the bed, pulling the pillow under my head and curling up on it, preparing for the sleep that's going to take me.

I'm trying to ignore her warnings about death as I stare upward at the vines that grow across my ceiling all the way from the window.

The bed dips as Slater moves up it to sit beside me. "You need to rest now. I'll watch over you."

He turns his back on me, facing the window. Guarding me.

I close my eyes and take stock of my current state of health, surprised to discover that I feel...

Fine.

Alert.

My eyes fly open and my forehead creases in confusion.

I sit up, expecting to feel faint. Dizzy. For my bed to beckon me back to it.

None of that happens.

"Emmaline, is everything okay?"

"More than okay," I whisper. "I don't feel tired at all."

For a moment, I wonder if the potion I drank has staved off my exhaustion, but I've drunk potions in advance of creating portals before and it didn't stop me from collapsing afterward.

"I maintained a protection spell *and* opened a portal, but I don't feel any side effects," I say, examining my hands as if the answers will present themselves there. "How is this possible?"

When I focus back on Slater, I find him staring at my neck. "Emmaline?"

"What is it?"

"Your choker is torn."

My hands fly to my throat. "No..."

Slipping off the bed, I hurry to the dressing table again, carefully stepping around the broken glass. I snatch up my handheld mirror off the table. It's cracked, but there's a large enough chunk of reflective glass for me to see what Slater meant.

Toward the left-hand side, the top edge of the lace is frayed and there's a little split about a quarter of an inch down into the material.

I've worn this choker for as long as I can remember, and it's never torn before. Never broken.

It's a symbol of my purity.

And now...

I fight the panic rising into my throat because I don't know what it means.

This tear can't be responsible for my lack of exhaustion. My choker is a symbol of my power. Tearing it would surely mean my power is breaking, not getting stronger. But there's no doubt that I feel energized and alive and—

Dark light flickers at the edge of my vision, dragging my attention away from the choker and back to Slater.

He hovers behind me, and the concern in his eyes hurts me.

"Emmaline, talk to me."

My heart is in my throat as I follow the thread of power from me to Slater, the way the shadows rise up around him the closer he stands to me, the magic between us connecting our bodies.

I'm not sure when I stopped noticing how much the darkness feeds on my pure light.

Except that now I realize I got it all wrong. So terribly wrong.

The darkness isn't feeding *on* my light.

It's *feeding* my light. Adding to it. Making me stronger.

It isn't leaping toward me like I thought it was.

I'm *calling* it to me.

I've been calling it since I first touched Slater in the desert.

Fallon was right. There's death between us. And now my choker is breaking because of the darkness I've been siphoning into my body.

I stumble back from Slater, my eyes wide, a cry rising to my throat. "How could I do this?"

Slater goes still, his hand outstretched toward me. "Emmaline!" he commands me again. "Talk to me!"

I try to speak past the constriction in my throat as I press hard against the edge of my dressing table.

"I should have listened to what my sisters said." I gasp for breath, my chest squeezing. "Any witch who understands the nature of your curse can access its power."

A wary light enters his eyes. "What are you saying?"

I'm forced to acknowledge the true nature of this impossible connection between us.

"I'm already doing it," I say. "I'm already draining you."

CHAPTER 23
SLATER

The anguish on Emmaline's face tears me apart. Tears fill her eyes as she slips around the table and backs away from me, heading toward the door. Her hand presses to her torn choker where the shadows grow.

"Am I turning toward darkness?" she asks.

I fight every instinct in my body that tells me to go after her, but it will only drive her further away because she thinks she'll hurt me.

I don't even have to ask myself is she could.

This careful, caring woman would never harm me.

In fact, quite the opposite. I've never felt so powerful as I do in her presence.

"If you were embracing darkness, you wouldn't give a fuck about hurting me," I say, trying to convey to her the strength of my conviction. "You wouldn't care that this power growing within me—whatever the hell it is—could kill me."

I take a step forward.

She takes a step back, her hand held out to ward me off. "No. Don't come closer."

All I want to do is wrap her up in my arms, but I force myself to stay where I am. "Even if you don't trust yourself right now, trust me when I tell you how I feel."

She glances at the door, and I know it won't take much for her to leave, but, hell, that would hurt me more.

I refuse to release her from my gaze, needing to make her understand. "I feel strong, Emmaline. I can hear, see, and sense so much more than I could before. If I took to the sky right now, I have no doubt I could fly faster, and that my reflexes would be quicker, than ever before. Every time you touch me—"

I take a deep breath, struggling to rein in the impact she has on me. "Every damn time. I feel like I come alive. Like I'm more alive than I've ever been."

She's stopped glancing at the door, and I dare to take another step forward, now standing in the wide space between the base of the bed and her dressing table.

This time, she doesn't move away from me.

"Please don't go, Emmaline."

She presses her hand to her heart as tears trickle down her cheeks. "What if this connection we feel is a lie?" she asks. "What if it's a mechanism to lull you into a false sense of safety to keep you under control?"

"Then, I wouldn't feel it with you," I say, with absolute certainty. "The curse-maker wouldn't have designed this curse so that I'd fall in love with *you*. My feelings for you will only make me fight harder against the curse-maker. I'll fight to be with you and to protect you. If loving someone is a side effect of this curse, then they would have designed it to make me love *them*."

Emmaline's breathing is ragged, coming in little gasps. She swipes at the teardrops that have made it to her chin.

Then her hand drops to the copper penny resting at her throat. "Love." She nearly sobs the word.

"Yes," I say, determined for her to believe it.

She squeezes her eyes closed, causing a final rush of tears to release down her cheeks. Her knuckles are turning white with how hard she's pressing her fist to her heart.

When she opens her eyes, I see her doubt, and it nearly breaks me.

"I've lived for sixty years and never fallen in love," she says. "I've only known you for a matter of days."

My jaw clenches. "You think it isn't possible to fall in love that fast." I cast my gaze around the room. "Two days ago, I didn't think my survival was possible. But here I am. Still breathing. And with every breath I take, I know that I need—"

My senses prickle, sharply enough to stop me mid-sentence.

My instinct to get Emmaline out of here is suddenly stronger than ever.

"Someone's coming," I say, every muscle in my body tense, my wings ready to spring wide.

She casts a wild look around the room. "I don't—"

Icy wind blasts through the room, snatching away her voice.

The curtains behind me billow and the vines across the wall suddenly freeze over. The shards of glass on the floor rise up like gems before they spear into the ceiling, sticking there. At the same time, the bed and dressing table both fold up like they're made of paper and flatten against the wall, clearing the floor of all furniture and opening up the space.

It fills with a storm of ice.

For a split second, I think the attack is coming from the window-side of the room.

But then two figures appear in a whirlwind beside Emmaline, who has jolted backward, her hands raised defensively.

The Crone and the Mother are both still dressed in black. The Crone is wearing her glamour again, her silver hair billowing around her thin form. She's the source of the icy air, which pours from her palms.

The Mother's eyes reflect amber flames that burn around her hands. All hints of her emerald irises are gone, her black hair accentuating the golden flames that rise up in front of her face.

She lifts her burning fists to her mouth and blows across them.

At the same time, the Crone releases the icy particles clinging to her fingers.

Fire and ice pour toward me.

I don't have time to experience shock.

My response is purely instinctive.

My wings shoot out, wrapping around my body. The lower half of my right wing is now covered entirely in white feathers and, with the emergence of my wings, white light bursts around me.

The blast of ice and fire raging toward me hits the protective surface that has shot up around me, rushing to either side in a deadly wash, as if seeking a way in.

"Stop!" Emmaline screams, spinning to her sisters. "What are you doing?"

"Trapping him!" the Mother cries, striding farther inside the room toward me. "We're out of time and it's the only way to stop the curse."

"Lower your shield, Emmaline," the Crone orders, standing closest to Emmaline now.

"I'm not..." Emmaline shakes her head. "I didn't..."

She stares at her hands, at the ebb and flow of dark light that dances between her and me. It's uninterrupted by the glistening but transparent shield that's protecting me, connecting us in a stream that flows back and forth.

It twines around her fingertips, two streams of light, bright and dark entangled like a piece of yarn.

It's increasingly difficult to see Emmaline clearly through the storm of magic—especially now that the Crone's icy power and the Mother's flames rush around me like a tornado, seeking a way in.

Through the wash, I hone in on Emmaline's lips as they part with her quickly indrawn breath.

I'm surprised by the sudden soft smile on her face. Her wide-eyed awe.

"I didn't create this shield." Her whisper would have

been drowned in the shrieking wind, except that my heightened senses allow me to hear it. "Which means we must be exchanging power. You're accessing my power to protect yourself."

She meets my eyes over the whirlwind of ice and fire.

I guess she was listening when I told her that my hearing is more sensitive now, because she continues at a whisper that her sisters won't be able to hear above the maelstrom. "I thought I was taking power from you, draining you... killing you... but I must have been giving it back, too. Power must have been flowing both ways."

No wonder I felt stronger.

"Giving on both sides," I say, wishing she could hear me as clearly as I hear her. "Like any good relationship."

"Emmaline!" the Crone cries. "You have to lower your shield!"

Clearly, the Crone doesn't see the power flowing between us—and didn't hear our conversation—since she still thinks Emmaline is protecting me.

"No!" Emmaline cries, making no effort to enlighten her sister. "Why must you trap him?"

"Because this curse has no cure," the Mother says. "And the curse-maker is coming. Sooner than we expected. They've already broken through our outer defenses."

The Mother isn't lying about the approach of a malevolent force.

The prickling sense of danger that I felt before the Crone and the Mother exploded into the room hasn't abated.

It's only getting worse.

I may not know who this curse-maker is, but their approach is like a scorching spot at the back of my mind. It feels like a spark, the kind that signals the start of a fire worse than the one already burning in this room, and there's no way in hell I'll let Emmaline perish in it.

"Maybe you should listen to your sisters," I whisper. "I don't want the curse-maker to use me against you."

If Emmaline hears me, it seems that she's choosing to ignore me this time because she doesn't respond.

Her jaw clenches. Her normally gentle eyes are wild and the dark light building around her is startling to behold.

I wish to fuck that her sisters could see the power gathered around her.

"Every curse has a cure," she snarls at them, her voice as savage as a wolf's growl, her eyes narrowed and glittering.

The Crone takes a hasty step away from Emmaline, the older witch's face paling.

It's hard to tell for sure through the wash of power, but it appears that the Crone's focus is suddenly drawn to the choker around Emmaline's neck. I'm sure I don't imagine her gasp.

"Your choker..." The Crone gives herself a savage shake. "Listen to me, Emmaline. This curse is more complex than any we've ever encountered. The energy source it's creating is already too far advanced to be reversed. There's nothing to be done but to suffocate it—"

"Suffocate it?" Emmaline jolts. "You mean suffocate *him*."

"It's the only way to ensure the curse doesn't latch on to one of us when he dies," the Mother says, circling toward me.

She and the Crone seem to be in sync now, both of them moving away from Emmaline, as if they intend to flank me.

"We must wipe his mind, destroy his raven, and leach the life from his body," the Crone says. "Then the curse will suffocate with him."

Emmaline is frozen where she stands facing me. She's all I care about, and right now, she's in as much danger as I am.

She stares from her hands to me, her gaze following the strands of power flowing back and forth between us, before she lifts her eyes to mine, a clash that takes my breath away.

Fuck.

The power growing around her carries the same wild heat she revealed to me in the grotto.

"We have no time, Emmaline." The Mother's fists are full of flames. "We must kill him. *Now*."

Emmaline raises her head high and, with her next inhale, I'm sure that the choker around her neck tears a little further, all on its own. Dark light flickers around her hand, turning the milky-white pearl on her ring to smoky gray.

Glaring at her sisters one at a time, she says, "You can fucking try."

CHAPTER 24
EMMALINE

My sisters respond to my challenge with dropped jaws and wide eyes. Their shock is possibly more about the fact that I cursed than the fact that I'm defying them, but I stand my ground.

I thought I was hurting Slater, but now I feel everything that I'm giving back to him. It's a maelstrom of power that ripples through me from my mind to my core, triggering every sensation imaginable.

Want. Fear. Pain. Strength. Pleasure. And beneath all that, a savage determination to hold on to what has been offered to me.

Him.

His heart and body.

My sisters are threatening his life, but so is the cursemaker.

If I know the Crone at all, she would have made her outer defenses the strongest to deter an attack. If the curse-maker has broken through those defenses, then it's only a matter of moments before they get through the rest.

The Crone recovers first. "Emmaline." Her stern voice doesn't allow any objection. "You will step aside and allow us to act."

"I won't."

She blinks at me.

I'm usually compliant. A perfect, pure maiden.

Not anymore.

"You don't have time to complete the suffocation spell," I say. "So either we fight each other, making ourselves vulnerable to the curse-maker, or we join forces against them. Which will it be?"

Before the Crone can reply, the air buzzes with power.

The Crone and the Mother both spin to face the window behind Slater moments before it explodes in crackling light that tears the window frame apart.

It's too late to change their minds now.

The curse-maker has arrived.

My sisters' power recedes from Slater as they rush toward each other on my left.

In the seconds that they're distracted, I take hold of the shield and use it to lift and propel Slater to the right-hand side of the room—opposite my sisters.

I sense his need to leap into the fight that's coming—I can see it in every tense muscle of his body and the way he focuses on the growing power in front of the broken window.

The worst thing he can do is make it easy for the curse-maker to access the power source they created.

"Stay where you are," I beseech him. "Don't give the curse-maker what they want."

His lips are pressed hard together—a sign that he doesn't like staying put—but he gives me a firm nod.

I don't yet understand how to use the combined power streaming through me, but I follow my instincts, allowing the magic to surge through my hands and thicken the glistening shield that's protecting him.

That's all I have time for before a form takes shape within the haze of power in front of the broken window opposite me.

It's a woman, clad in black leather pants and a halter-neck bodice. Her hair is glistening brown streaked with red and falls in long, straight strands to her waist. She has a strong jaw with a cleft in it. Her eyebrows and eyelashes are blood-red, and her eyes are the darkest brown.

She glitters with power.

"Well, what a cozy room," she says, her gaze traveling across the remnants of the vines decorating the walls to the shards of lavender vials that are stuck into the ceiling.

Her focus lands on the Crone. "Very different to the place you left me in, isn't it, Ethna?"

This woman knows the Crone?

Ethna's face has drained of color and both she and the Mother have lowered their hands.

"Adeline?" the Mother asks, her voice barely above a whisper. "Is that you?"

The woman—whose name is apparently Adeline—twirls her finger in the air, her power sparking as she moves. "I'm surprised you recognize me, Mother. I've changed a lot since you abandoned me."

The Mother's emerald eyes are wide. "We didn't abandon you. We had no choice."

Adeline tips her head. "Hmm, you clearly didn't care enough about me to bring me with you, so I'd call that abandonment, wouldn't you?"

The Crone seems to find her voice. "We couldn't risk—"

"That I would turn out like my mother?" Adeline laughs. It's a harsh sound. "You assumed she would mold me in her image once you were gone. But, you see, that would require that *she* cared about me, too."

As she speaks, Adeline takes careful steps toward me, approaching at a prowl. The closer she comes to me, the more I draw on Slater's heightened senses. Without his power, I would still know that this woman is a witch, but I'm certain I wouldn't discern the full depth of the myriad of glittering lights that swill around her.

She appears to control a confusing mix of powers, some of them conflicting. I sense multiple elemental powers, along with astral energy. It shouldn't be possible for one witch to control this many disparate powers, but it would explain how she got through the Crone's defenses so fast.

This woman is a formidable enemy.

"I was simply another plaything for my mother," Adeline continues while she places one foot carefully in front of the other. "A toy over which she had complete control. After all, who would come to the rescue of the cruel Queen's daughter?"

She flashes a narrow-eyed glare at the Crone. "Nobody. That's fucking who."

My focus flickers over my sisters, who are both pale and appear more uncertain than I've ever seen them. I'm not sure if they can discern all of the powers this woman controls, but I'm certain that Slater can.

He has remained on edge at the side of the room, his muscles visibly tense, and I sense through our combined power his instinct to spread his wings and fly at Adeline.

Oddly, Adeline hasn't paid any attention to him, which is even more confusing, given that Adeline must be the curse-maker. Surely, she's come to claim the power she has created?

"Who the hell are you?" I ask her, standing my ground. "And I don't mean your name."

Adeline pulls up sharply, re-appraising me. "The Maiden speaks." She widens her eyes at me. "And not as politely as her position requires."

Her eyes narrow at my neck and I can only imagine that my choker has caught her interest. A slow smile breaks across her face. "Although it seems you're breaking free of your chains."

She may be my enemy, but she speaks the truth about that.

I am breaking free.

For better or for worse.

A sudden sense of calm overtakes me. I ask again, more softly this time, "Who are you?"

Her gaze runs the length of my body and, although I'm certain my sisters don't see the shadows around me, it's clear that Adeline does when she follows the ribbon of darkness swirling from my legs up to my shoulders. "The more important question is: Who *was* I?" she says, casting another glare at my sisters. "Will you tell her, or will I?"

The Crone is tight-lipped, but the Mother's shoulders are hunched.

"Adeline was one of us," the Mother whispers.

"That's right," Adeline croons. "I was once *you*, Emmaline. One of The Three. I was their Maiden before you."

I've never been good at hiding what I feel, and I don't fight my surprise at this news. I suppose I assumed that they formed our coven once I'd joined it.

Adeline's expression softens and if I didn't know better, I'd suspect she views me with pity.

"You wouldn't believe it to look at me now," she says, "but I was once pure like you. Dedicated. *Kind*. I helped my people instead of imprisoning them. I was bound to serve the former Queen, who ruled benevolently."

While the Mother has remained pale, the Crone rallies much faster. "Then you conspired with your mother to slaughter the Queen and turn the old country to darkness."

"I had nothing to do with my mother's crimes!"

Adeline snarls. "She used me! But you were never going to believe that."

"Well, we were right," the Crone snaps. "Look at you now."

Adeline abandons her contemplation of me and strides toward the Crone. "You left me there to suffer!" she screams. "Well, now it's your turn."

She spins back to me, her power gathering in ribbons of light that I'm sure she's about to throw at me.

Behind her, the Crone whispers in the ancient language and glittering icicles as sharp as steel blades fly toward Adeline's back.

The second that they touch her, Adeline's body flickers, becoming ghostly and transparent, and the projectiles fly right through her without leaving a mark.

They hit the wall to my right, making rapid thudding sounds in the sudden silence.

Adeline laughs again, a sound that carries power. "You can't hurt me, Crone, because I'm not really there with you," she says. "I'm merely a projection."

"From where?" the Mother asks.

"From the other side of the portal," Adeline replies. "You can't hurt me unless you come for me. But, oh, I can hurt you."

The Mother and the Crone exchange a quick, alarmed look. If Adeline has remained on her side of the portal, then I suppose this explains why they didn't sense the arrival of a new supernatural being into this world. I imagine Adeline would have been smart enough to conceal her power even in astral form, so my sisters would not have detected her energy, either.

"How are you doing this?" the Crone demands to know. "You never had the power of astral-projection."

"I have many powers now," Adeline says. "The raven shifter isn't the first supernatural being whose power I've cultivated and harvested." She glides her hand through the air, leaving a trail of elemental powers behind: sunlight, frost, fire, even shadows like mine...

She snaps her fingers and the broken vines twining across the ceiling sprout flowers.

Black roses.

The vines begin to grow before my eyes, creeping across the ceiling and down the walls, snaking toward me and my sisters.

At the same time, the air around me becomes heavy, like a weight pushing me to the floor. The harder I fight to remain upright, the heavier the weight becomes.

Both the Mother and the Crone raise their hands, ice and fire hitting the vines in turn, but their knees buckle, their arms tremble, and sweat breaks out across their faces. I'm sure they're feeling the same weight I am when they drop to their knees.

My own knees hit the floor.

"Every witch and warlock I've harvested has given me their powers," Adeline says, deep concentration filling her eyes as she presses her finger to her lips. "Shh, don't tell my mother. She thinks I'm still pitifully *good*."

"Why are you here, Adeline?" the Mother asks. "Do

you intend to open another portal to the old country? Will you allow your mother to enslave this world too?"

Adeline stiffens. "Have you heard nothing I've said?" She punctuates her speech as she continues. "I'm not here to help my mother."

She takes a deep breath and appears to calm herself before she points at me. "I'm here for Emmaline."

My brow creases. Surely, she means she's here for Slater.

Adeline's focus flickers to him for a second, as if she reads my mind. "You thought I came for the raven?"

At the side of the room, Slater has spread his wings as if he were fighting the instinct to fly out of the protective sphere. Black vines are sliding across them, disappearing in the dark plumage but stark against the white feathers, dragging him back against the wall.

Adeline drops to her knees in front of me, blocking my view of Slater, while her vines creep closer to my legs like chains threatening to bind me.

The air buzzes around me, a new influx of magic. At the side of the room, the Mother and the Crone are slumped against the floor, but they suddenly crane forward in a way that makes me think they can't hear us now. Adeline must be using some sort of spell to conceal our conversation.

Adeline confirms it when she says, "The others can't hear us now."

She continues softly. "The raven shifter is my gift to you, Emmaline. A message from the world you left behind."

"You can't make a gift of a person's life," I say. "What you're doing is murder."

The malice clears from her expression and for a brief moment, I recognize the Maiden she once was. Guileless. Honest. Sincere.

"It's cruel, I know." She nods. "But I won't abandon you to die like Ethna and Eugenia abandoned me. I'm giving you a chance to survive."

She takes a deep breath. "You see, I made a deal with my mother."

"What deal?" I ask, my question stiff as I fight the increasing pressure on my vocal chords.

"If I kill you, she will name me her successor and seal it in blood. When she dies, I will be Queen." Adeline holds up her forefinger. "But your death must be witnessed by our people. It must be publicly beheld. The hope your existence gives them must be crushed once and for all."

My brow furrows. What hope could my existence give to the people of the old country? Except perhaps if I were to use my power as the Maiden... Perhaps to drive out darkness and bring balance...

Adeline's lips stretch into a thin smile. "My mother has been trying to lure you back for years. Until you're dead, she will never be completely in control, and the whispers of your return will continue."

Adeline widens her eyes at me. "Oh, the schemes she's come up with over the years. Believe me, this path is the lesser of all the evils."

She stands up and the air *pops* around my ears. The

spell she was using to conceal our conversation must have broken.

Sounds rush in... The Mother groans as she struggles to crawl across the floor toward me. The Crone's power hisses as icicles form across her skin, as if she's trying to push back against the weight on her shoulders. Slater is quiet and my fear for him grows, but Adeline is still blocking my view.

She towers over me, pure darkness once more, as she declares, "Sixty years ago, my mother killed your mother. Come fight me for your birthright, Emmaline." Her smile fades. "*I challenge you.*"

My mind is in turmoil. Everything Adeline says washes over me, a buzz of sound, as I try to connect the pieces about my past.

I knew that the cruel Queen murdered my family, but my family were regular witches and warlocks. Now, Adeline is implying that my family... That my mother... was more than I thought. That I have a birthright that must be fought for and claimed.

But I also know that I shouldn't trust Adeline or anything she says. All of it could be designed to hurt me, my sisters, and Slater.

Behind her, the Mother's cheeks are draining pale again.

Adeline barely acknowledges the Mother before she says, "Don't look so shocked, Mother. You knew this day would come. Emmaline is a loose thread that my mother wants cut." Her forehead creases. "Or is that burned? Frayed? Whatever. Emmaline has to die."

"And what then?" the Mother asks.

"Then I will have proven myself worthy as her successor." Adeline reaches for me, a single finger as if she would hook it beneath my chin, but she stops short of touching me. "All I have to do is kill her in front of our people. Then I'll be the rightful heir."

It's the second time she's said she needs to kill me publicly, but the Mother and the Crone couldn't hear her before, so I have no doubt her declaration is intended to upset them now.

The muscles in the Crone's neck strain as she fights to lift her head. "You're deluded if you think Augusta will ever hand over the throne to you," she snaps, "She'll do everything in her power to extend her own life beyond its natural limits."

"You'll be waiting a long time for her to die," the Mother concurs, her fingers clawed against the floor.

"No," Adeline whispers, looking down at me, speaking directly to me. "At the moment of your death, I will siphon your life force—and through you, the life force of the shifter. In that moment, I will finally have enough power to kill my mother."

Adeline's expression becomes as hard as stone. "She will die screaming at my hands for all the pain she has inflicted. The question is, Maiden: How will *you* die?"

Her voice lowers. "Will you live out your life like a coward, hiding in your perfect little haven while your people suffer? Or will you come and fight me and die with honor?"

My heart is in my throat and I'm struggling to unpick

the emotions I'm feeling. A deep anger, but mostly a need for answers, because of all the information about my family that my sisters seem to have kept from me.

Adeline glares at them once more. "Just in case you're considering advising Emmaline to avoid this fight, remember that I can come back at any time and harvest the shifter's life force. And yes, I will use the power to hurt this world. The explosion I caused in Dublin when I cursed the shifter will be nothing compared to—"

A shadow passes over her from behind.

She whirls.

But not before a wing cuts through her body. Black and white feathers gleam like onyx and diamonds. They spark as they connect with her form and rivers of fire are suddenly set alight across her skin.

Her eyes fly wide, and she screams.

It's a sound of real pain.

Her cry fades as her projection disappears and finally, the weight lifts from my shoulders. The black vines stop growing, freezing in place, although they don't disappear like Adeline did.

Slater drops to his knees in front of me. "Emmaline! Are you okay?"

"Slater." I look up at him, reaching for him. I can't put into words how I'm feeling. *I'm fine* seems inadequate when a new weight is crashing down on me.

It's the heaviness of uncertainty and a sense of responsibility.

I have questions for my sisters. So many questions.

Slater helps me to my feet before he pulls me close. "Well, now I know who cursed me."

On my left, both the Mother and the Crone are lifting themselves up, their hands trembling, their shoulders hunched and their chests heaving as they draw audibly deep breaths.

They must have been fighting with all their strength against Adeline's immense power—a power that she could have used to kill us on the spot, but she seems determined to carry through with her plan.

I need to know the truth about my family.

Turning within Slater's arms, I face my sisters with a demand for answers. "What have you been keeping from me?"

CHAPTER 25
SLATER

E mmaline's voice is quiet, but the power thrumming through her is as wild as waves in a rocky sea.

She could sweep me up and drown me. All of us, in fact.

Much of her conversation with the curse-maker—Adeline—was concealed from me, but the ultimate message was clear: Adeline intends to draw Emmaline back to her birth country and destroy her. Whatever Adeline said about me, I didn't hear it, but it's clear I'm some kind of pawn in this game.

My own rage is a storm that I fight to control. The flow of power now rushing between me and Emmaline is overwhelming in its intensity. I try to rein it in, to clamp down on my emotions. I tell myself to remain calm.

No matter what Emmaline needs me to do, I'm here for her. And right now, I sense she needs all the calm she can get.

Her sisters appear drained, their expressions ashen. The Crone rubs her temples, and the Mother leans up against the wall behind her, her black dress and dark hair making her drawn features stand out against the backdrop of black vines.

"We need to talk," the Mother replies quietly. "We need to explain everything. But not here. Emmaline, let's go to your garden, where we can get some fresh air."

She's stalling and Emmaline isn't having any of it. "A change of environment won't alter my question."

"I know," the Mother says, blinking hard against the glisten of tears in her eyes. "But it will help us give you the answers you need."

Emmaline is tense in my arms, but her shoulders sag a little, her power softens, and she seems to capitulate.

She gives a soft sigh. "Okay. There are potions in my garden that will help you regain your energy."

She leads the way, pausing beside the door, where she dropped the satchel earlier. It contains the bundle of my lost feathers.

When she lifts the flap, it's half full of feathers. The visible ones flutter in the breeze from the broken window. It's clear that the feathers I've lost since I plucked the first ten from the Tree of Lost Things have appeared within the satchel. Although it looks like they aren't bundled within the ribbon that subdues their power. That fact is confirmed when heat rises off them, seemingly triggered by the nearness of Emmaline's hand.

She drops the flap and slips the satchel over her shoulder.

The Crone and the Mother support each other as they step out after her. They're both clearly struggling, although the Mother seems worse off than the Crone.

I don't expect the Mother to accept my assistance, but I offer anyway. "May I help you walk?"

The Mother's green eyes are dull as she turns them up to me. She doesn't say anything as she steps toward me, reaching out.

I'm surprised she accepted my help, but I immediately hook my arm around her torso, supporting her.

The Crone gives me a shallow nod that feels like a reluctant acknowledgment. Now that she's not trying to help the Mother, she walks a little more upright.

We follow Emmaline in silence, but I'm aware of her frequent glances back and the way her eyes fill when she sees the Mother leaning on me. Emmaline may be angry with her sisters, but she's clearly concerned for their wellbeing.

The silence gives me time to process some of what we learned from Adeline. She said she was the one who created the explosion in the pub in Dublin. At the time, Vesperus found out that one of his enemies had hired a witch to make the explosion, but we didn't discover the witch's identity. Now, I know who she is, although it's still unclear to me why she chose to curse *me* in particular and not one of the others at the pub.

Ahead of me, Emmaline pauses as she steps from the glass room into the outdoors, her head tipped back toward the sky.

Her garden is her home and it's precious to her. It appears to be intact, but the sky is not.

Gray clouds have gathered over the previously perfect sky, obscuring the pristine blue and the bright sunlight. The dark pall crackles up ahead, and my senses pick up the broken magic that hovers high above us. Adeline must have destroyed layers of illusion and magical protections to get to us.

Emmaline squares her shoulders and gathers herself before she strides ahead of us along the path with flowery bushes. She quickly gathers vials of potions before she heads to the open grassy patch on the right-hand side of the garden.

"Come and sit," she says, and neither of her sisters objects.

I help the Mother to the center of the open area, where she sinks to the ground.

The Crone stays close to the Mother, both of them giving grateful sighs when Emmaline hands them a mix of colorful vials. Red and golden like the potions she gave me for pain and healing, along with lavender for energy, like the vial she drank when she thought she would collapse after opening the portal to the Gold and Garnet headquarters.

She also hands them a green vial each, but I'm not sure what that's for.

Her sisters quickly drink each potion except the green one, which they turn over in their palms, their expressions closed off.

Emmaline gives them each a hard look as she sits opposite them.

"For courage," she says.

The Mother takes a deep breath and places the vial onto the grass in front of her. "Truth should be faced, even if it's painful," she says. "There is no taking the edge off this."

The Crone folds her hands in her lap. The color is returning to her cheeks, and I sense that her power is returning with her renewed health.

I'm shocked when her eyes glisten with tears like the Mother's. The Crone hasn't treated me kindly, but the pain in her expression right now couldn't be faked.

She doesn't shy away from Emmaline's intense gaze as she begins to speak. "Adeline was the best of us. Kinder and gentler than any Maiden we could have hoped for. She balanced our trio. But because we loved her so much, we didn't see past her to the shadow that stood behind her. We didn't see what her mother, Augusta, was becoming."

"A dark witch," the Mother whispers. "As if nature were trying to balance itself out. All of Adeline's goodness versus all of her mother's cruelty."

"There were signs," the Crone says. "Young witches were becoming ill and several died. Three of the Queen's hounds turned rabid and attacked a group of warlocks, killing two. The spreading oak tree in the Queen's garden began to rot and we couldn't find the cause."

She stops speaking, and the Mother picks up the story. "We were the Queen's advisors, so we had direct access to her. In fact, one of us was always with her. As you would expect in a land of witches and warlocks, there was always the threat of a magical attack, so we guarded her."

She pauses, taking a deep breath before she continues. "One night, Adeline's mother wore a glamour. She impersonated Adeline, infiltrated the Queen's quarters, and killed the Queen. Augusta made sure she was seen doing it and in so doing, falsely implicated Adeline in the murder."

"Wearing another witch's face is strictly forbidden for this very reason," the Crone says. "Adeline was distraught. She swore it wasn't her, but we didn't have time to take the steps to find out for sure. Augusta quickly took control of the palace with the help of a group of warlocks, and in the chaos that followed, we had to flee." She sighs. "Without Adeline."

"I suppose that was another cruel step in Augusta's plan," the Mother says. "She not only assassinated the Queen, but destroyed her own daughter in the process."

"A daughter whose power she hated." The Crone hasn't looked away, but new tears brim in her blue eyes before she swipes at them. "You were with me that night, Emmaline. You had a fever, and I was trying to make a potion, but I was never very good at the damn things. I don't have the natural talent for them that you do."

She picks up the green vial, the one for courage, and turns it over in her hands. "Your mother didn't want to leave you that night, but I insisted she should get some rest. It's my fault she was vulnerable."

Emmaline has listened quietly, but now she whispers, "My mother... The Queen."

The Crone gives her a firm nod. "We took you and ran."

"We traveled the underground passageway to the portal and came through to the other side before Augusta's new guards could stop us," the Mother says.

"We never looked back," the Crone finishes.

Emmaline is intensely quiet, but once again, I sense her rising power. When I woke up in the cell, I suspected that she didn't realize how much power she controls, but I believe she's becoming more aware with every passing minute.

She looks up. "So Adeline wasn't lying. I'm the former Queen's daughter."

"You are," the Crone says. "The only living heir to the throne."

CHAPTER 26

SLATER

E mmaline stares at her hands and I sense a
dangerous rush of power from me to her, as if
she's pulling on the tether between us like a
lifeline.

"Is Emmaline the name my mother gave me?" she
asks.

The Crone is quiet and it's the Mother who answers,
although hesitantly. "Emmaline is your Maiden name.
The Queen called you 'Raven' for your dark hair."

A bitter moan leaves Emmaline's lips. "Raven?"

I stiffen where I stand beside her, my wings tucked to
my sides. It doesn't escape me that of all the supernatural
beings Adeline could have chosen to curse, she chose me,
one of a small number of raven shifters left alive after the
Great Sacrifice.

Emmaline looks up at me, the power pulling and
pulling between us with every breath she takes.

"She told me she was trying to send me a message,"

Emmaline whispers. "She cursed you, knowing you would seek me out—seek this coven out—in a bid to save your life. But I didn't know enough about myself to understand why she would send a *raven* to find me." She grips her stomach with a moan. "She sent you, a raven, with the threat of death hanging over your head. I think she intended you as a symbol for me and the death she wants hanging over *my* head."

I want to reach for her, but the air is charged between us.

Painfully so.

The choker around her neck is a few threads away from breaking apart and with every pull of power between us, the lace bracelet she's wearing is fraying at the edges too.

She drags in a breath and pins her sisters with her hard gaze. "You always told me that the current Queen of the old country is brutal. That witches and warlocks tried to escape her. But you never told me I had a responsibility to stop her."

The Crone's eyes are widening. "You can't be thinking of accepting Adeline's challenge—"

"People are suffering!" Emmaline's response is a near shout. "You let it go on."

"No, Emmaline." The Crone reaches for her. "You can't stop any of this. *We* couldn't stop any of it. You're the Maiden—"

"So is Adeline."

"It's not the same," the Crone says. "Adeline has siphoned the powers of other witches and warlocks to make herself more powerful. She has challenged you by the blood of the people you want to protect. If you go..."

The Crone's voice breaks. Her hand flies across her mouth, as if she could contain her sorrow. "If you return to the old country to fight Adeline, you'll die. I don't... I can't... lose you..."

I never imagined I'd witness tears flowing freely down the Crone's face, but from what they've said, she and the Mother raised Emmaline from when she was a baby.

They are her family.

Emmaline's eyes are now brimming too. The stream of power between us carries her grief to me, but it also carries her determination.

Shadows build around her hands and, at the same time, a glow emanates from within the satchel beside her. My feathers must be heating up, and I can only guess they're responding to the influx of energy swirling between Emmaline and me.

I want to wrap Emmaline up in my arms and tell her we'll find another way to defeat Adeline, but the Mother speaks before I can make a move.

"We have to let her go," the Mother says quietly.

The Crone swivels to the Mother, her eyes shooting wide. "How can you say that? We've protected Emmaline all her life. We've kept her safe from the monsters of her past. We can't let her go back. Not ever."

The Mother reaches for the Crone's hand, and I'm struck by how much these two witches care about Emmaline. The lengths they'd go to protect her. They lengths they *have* gone to keep her safe.

"We can," the Mother says. "Because she's strong enough."

The Crone's forehead furrows deeply. "Emmaline can't fight Adeline, let alone her mother. She was born with a Maiden's power. It was written in the fates."

The Mother blows out a soft breath. "Actually... that isn't entirely true."

The Crone stares at the Mother for a long, charged moment.

Neither of them speaks while the Mother's eyes fill with fresh tears and the Crone's lips press into a worried line.

Emmaline has remained tense where she sits on the ground beside me, her gaze now flying back and forth between the two women, but she also remains silent, her hands pressed against her thighs, as if she's prepared to wait for them to speak.

The Crone finally breaks the silence with a trembling whisper. "What did you do, Eugenia?"

The Mother reaches for her left wrist, where she wears the bracelet made of three entwined threads.

I first noticed it when I woke up in the cell beneath their castle and my power was fully heightened for the first time. I suspected at the time that Emmaline and the Crone couldn't see this bracelet because of the concealment spell I detected around it.

The three threads are exactly like the threads that I followed to find these women—my lifeline through the desert. They are three distinct magics wound around each other, each filament glittering with the strength of magic that I associate with each of them: the Crone's wrath, the Mother's wisdom, and the Maiden's purity.

Now, the Mother waves her hand gently across the air above the bracelet and I sense the concealment spell break.

It's clear that the bracelet is now visible to both Emmaline and the Crone when they gasp.

"Fates!" Emmaline exclaims. "Why are you wearing them?"

"They're yours," the Mother says.

Emmaline jolts back while the furrow in the Crone's forehead only deepens.

"Explain this to me," Emmaline orders the Mother, her power rising again.

The lace bracelet around Emmaline's wrist frays even further as she speaks, but I'm not sure she notices.

"After we came to this world, on the day of your first birthday, the thread of your fate split into three," the Mother says, speaking carefully. "Each strand carried a different power."

I can't stay quiet. "Maiden, Mother, Crone," I say, the words rumbling off my tongue.

The Mother acknowledges me with a nod. "That's right." Her eyes gleam with the tears she isn't allowing to fall. "Emmaline was fated to the life of all three. A power never before seen."

Emmaline is frozen where she sits, and I drop to my

knees beside her, offering the comfort of my nearness if she wants it.

The Mother's voice is barely audible as she continues. "A power like that shouldn't exist, so I did something unthinkable and... unforgivable..."

The Crone is pale. "Eugenia?"

The Mother swallows visibly. "I tied off the threads at the point before they split, and also at the three loose ends, forming two knots. I used my power over flame to solder the two knots together so that the three threads formed a loop. And then..."

She's shaking so hard, it seems she can't speak now.

Emmaline grips my arm as if she needs an anchor as she waits for the Mother to continue. "What did you do, Mother?"

"I cut off the loop," the Mother whispers, pointing to the bracelet she's wearing. "I wrapped the threads around my wrist and concealed them. And then I cut off the Crone and Mother threads that were already regrowing beyond the two knots, leaving only the Maiden's fate to continue thriving."

The Crone's eyes are wide, her shock palpable. "You cut Emmaline's fates? You could have killed her!"

"No," the Mother insists. "It's the only way to cut out unwanted sections of fate without killing someone."

"*Unwanted* sections?" Emmaline asks, her voice seething.

"There's more," the Mother says.

Emmaline closes her eyes, as if more will be too

much. Her jaw clenches before she opens her eyes again. "Tell me."

"It happened when we visited the Fire and Fluorite headquarters," the Mother says, her voice quavering. "When we came home, I discovered that your fate had split into three again. But this time, it was too late to constrain the threads. While we were away, they must have taken on a life of their own. Their power stretched up from the tapestry, across the ceiling, and out into the corridor beyond.

"I placed a concealment spell over them to hide them within our haven—the most powerful spell I could conjure—but there was no restraining them beyond that. They were already reaching out toward something... or maybe... *someone*."

There's a question in the Mother's eyes when she looks over at me.

I give her a nod. "I followed the threads here. I thought they belonged to each of you."

Emmaline catches her breath. "They wrapped around your throat when I first saw you. They dragged you to me."

"Fated," I say, surer than ever that my destiny lies with Emmaline. "I'm fated to give you the strength you need to fight the battle that's awaiting you."

Emmaline's anger fades and now she looks empty.

The shadows vanish from around her hands and so does the heat from the feathers in the satchel.

She presses a finger to the simple penny around her

neck. She doesn't speak aloud what the penny represents, but I know it: *love*.

"Adeline told me you were a gift," she whispers. "But my fates chose you to be much more to me."

I reach out to brush away the tear trickling down her cheek. "We found each other."

She gives me a heartbreaking smile as her focus shifts to the Tree of Lost Things behind me.

Then back to me. "All this time, *I* was the lost thing."

CHAPTER 27
EMMALINE

I can't make this choice.

And yet... I don't really *have* a choice.

If I don't accept Adeline's challenge, she'll come back and claim Slater's life, using the power within him to wreak hell upon this world.

To stop her, I would have to fight her.

But if I'm going to fight her, then I should do it far away from this world that I've worked hard to keep safe. In a place where I have the chance to get close to the witch who killed my family: Adeline's mother.

I've never killed anyone in my life, but then, I've always maintained my Maiden powers of peace, heart, and purity.

The Crone's power on the other hand...

Well, the Crone deals in death, and the Mother has the wisdom to know when delivering death is the only choice.

I was destined to be all three at once and I'm ready to embrace all of the power that was meant to be mine.

I rise to my feet and Slater follows me, his wings slightly spread. The bottom half of his left wing is completely white, and now the feathers on the bottom half of his right wing are starting to turn white too.

The Mother and the Crone slowly rise, wobbling and supporting each other as they find their feet.

They've always been strong—they're both powerful women—but they're not heartless. Far from it. Reliving the past appears to have drained them beyond what any potion can cure.

I can't imagine the pain they felt when they lost their Queen and their former Maiden, and fled their home country to keep me alive.

As much as I wish it weren't so, past trauma can't simply be magicked away.

"I don't have much time," I say. "I don't want Adeline to become impatient and launch an attack. In the short time that I have left, I need you to teach me what you can."

The Crone smooths down her black dress. She gives me a firm nod. "I can slow the passage of time here a little more than usual. While I'm doing that, you can start with Eugenia's powers. Then I'll teach you all I can about being a Crone."

She pauses before she turns away. "I'll also create a transportation system directly to the portal in the Sahara, so you don't need to expend energy traveling to it."

I hold my tongue before I tell her that I can open

temporary portals now without paying a price. I would use up energy doing so, and it's far better for me to conserve my power for the encounter with Adeline, so I accept her offer.

"Thank you," I say.

The Crone squeezes the Mother's hand before she hurries away in the direction of the castle. Above us, the artificial sky is cracked, and energy sizzles through the air. The illusion of the forest that conceals the castle is darkened by clouds. It appears as if the Crone disappears between the shadowy trees when really, she's entering the castle.

Slater is quick to step to my side. "How can I help?"

I take a deep breath, pushing away the fear and uncertainty threatening to paralyze me. "I need you to gather some of my potions."

I list off the colors of the potions I need, including hydration potions and pain relievers, asking for two of each.

Slater gives me a nod and sets off into the garden toward the Tree of Lost Things, leaving me with the Mother.

She clasps her hands in front of herself. "I won't ask for your forgiveness," she says. "Because what I did was reprehensible. I only ask that you fight as hard as you can to stay alive because without you..."

Her emerald eyes glisten, and I feel the depth of her love for me within my heart. She may believe I can't forgive her, but I already have.

"Without you, we are not whole," she says.

I bite back my fears and sadness as I sink back to the grass beside the satchel containing Slater's lost feathers.

The Mother joins me, sitting directly opposite me and closer than before.

I consider her carefully, my forehead creased, as I contemplate what I already know about her abilities, along with the sense of my own fledgling Mother power. "You have the ability to read the fates. And the wisdom to understand how a change in fate can influence future events."

She nods, a slow movement. "That's correct."

I give her a small smile. "Then... you must have known how all this would turn out."

She inhales a sharp breath. Then stares back at me, holding her breath for a long moment before she exhales. "Yes."

I shake my head, suppressing a wry laugh. "What I wonder about is if you hadn't looped my fates and cut them—would I have become who I am?"

Her only answer is a mysterious smile. "You tell me."

When I remain quiet, she reaches for my hands.

"The light inside you was always stronger than the darkness," she says, "but darkness consumes light too easily. Hatred and negativity are rapid emotions that strike fast and can quickly consume us. Kindness takes thought. It takes time and effort. Compassion is by far the hardest emotion to sustain. Your heart needed the chance to thrive. To experience hope and love undamaged by the horrors of your past."

Her hands tighten around mine. "Of course, that did

not mean keeping you unaware of darkness or naïve about its effects. No. Only through understanding pain can you truly know the power of compassion."

She leans toward me. "A Crone's power is in her strength. A Mother's power is in her wisdom. Compassion builds both."

I consider what she said. "You didn't really stifle my Crone or Mother powers, did you?"

She gives a firm shake of her head. "Well, I mean... you didn't have the opportunity to study the tapestry like I did or learn the spells you would have learned as a Crone, but you're as wise as I am and as strong as Ethna."

I'm not so convinced. "Really?"

Her smile broadens. "You can turn a poisonous belladonna seed into a sunflower at the touch of your hand." She arches an eyebrow at me. "I imagine that you even transformed a thread of fates that had wrapped around a certain shifter's throat into something harmless. Simple rope, perhaps? Am I wrong?"

I bite my lip as I remember my surprise when the rope had simply fallen away from Slater's neck at my touch.

"The Crone has studied for years to perfect her powers of transformation," the Mother says. "And you perform such magic by instinct alone. Driven by your need to render a harmful thing harmless. And *that*, Emmaline, is the power of compassion."

I close my eyes and exhale the storm of emotions building within me, forcing myself to face the sensation that could be my downfall. "I'm afraid."

"Of death?"

I shake my head, seeking Slater across the distance. "Of the pain my death would cause."

"Then you must fight with everything you have to stay alive," the Mother says, drawing my focus back to her. "Your protective instincts are your greatest strength. By protecting Slater, you will protect yourself."

I consider her advice carefully, but it all feels far more complicated than it sounds.

The Mother reaches for the satchel with the feathers in it. "I wonder if I might teach you a little about fire?" she asks, pulling the satchel into her lap.

I give her a quick nod. "Okay."

"Fire represents the power of the heart." She lifts the flap on the satchel and the feathers within it instantly begin to glow. "It takes a long time to master power over flames safely. The Crone will be able to tell you stories of all the mishaps I had when I was learning to control mine." The Mother gives me a wink. "Luckily, she was there to put out the worst of the blazes I started."

She reaches for the topmost feather, its black tendrils nearly touching her palm before she pauses.

"Dear fates, that's hot," she says, flashing a grin between me and Slater. He's wading into a row of bushes at the end of the path and reaching into a patch of orange tulips. When he can't reach the flower he wants, he spreads his wings, rises upward, and floats above the greenery, deftly plucking out the vial he was aiming for.

Every move he makes is smooth and when he lifts back up, beating his wings and rising into the air, I remember the way he said he thought he could fly faster now. Even from across the distance, I sense the tension in his muscles, as if he's reining in his desire to fly higher, before he touches down again.

My cheeks flush at the Mother's teasing tone. "Why are the feathers reacting this way?"

She looks at me expectantly. "Do you have any theories?"

I'm sure she's testing me now, so I work through it in my mind and verbalize my thoughts. "Well... Every time another one of Slater's feathers turns white, the black one ends up in a place where I'll find it. First, they appeared on the Tree of Lost Things and now they're gathering in the satchel. I thought it was part of the curse, but now I'm not so sure... Could it be a transference of energy?"

Her smile tells me I'm on the right track. "A cursed feather would die, but Slater is fighting back," she says. "His body has the ability to regrow feathers, so that's what he's doing. Just not in the ordinary way."

I consider her theory and summarize it. "So each time a feather turns white under the force of the curse, the spark of life in it manifests into a new feather."

"And each feather contains the spark of new life," the Mother replies. "Which he's giving to you."

I hover my hand above the feathers, close to the Mother's hand. "Each one contains power."

"The power of heart." Her green eyes glow with the fire of her own strength. "Which you can command."

My brow furrows. "I don't know how..."

"Start small," she suggests. "Get one to levitate."

Now I shake my head firmly. "I don't have that power. I certainly don't know the spell."

Her smile is gentle. "Spells are simply carefully curated words that form a conduit between a witch's power and their intentions. Spells have been handed down through generations because a particular form of words has proven to have the intended outcome without unwanted side effects."

She holds up a cautionary finger. "Now, of course, if you don't have the power to accomplish a thing, then it doesn't matter how many times you utter a spell. I can't, for example, turn these feathers into ice because that isn't my power. But you, Emmaline. *Oh*." She breaks into a smile again. "Your power could be limitless."

Chewing on my lip, I draw on the force within me while I focus on the feather sitting on the top of the pile.

"Lift," I whisper.

Nothing happens.

"Lift," I command more loudly.

Opposite me, the Mother clears her throat.

I glance up to discover her wobbling in the air, her legs still folded, her palms pressing down against the space at her sides as if she's trying to balance on air alone.

"Details are important," she says pointedly.

"Oops." I grimace. "Stop lifting?"

The Mother drops to the ground, and I sense her using her own power to slow her descent so she won't bruise.

This time, I choose my words more carefully. I imagine that the feather is a portal and I want it to take me somewhere, making a request of it the same way that I would open a portal.

"Little black feather," I whisper. "Please lift into the air where you can feel the breeze and remember what it was like to fly."

The feather ruffles before it rises, lifting out of the satchel and upward until it floats at my eye level.

"I did it," I say, astonished that it actually worked.

The feather twirls slowly, gliding back and forth in front of me, its tip smoldering with growing heat. I sense the energy within it, trapped and waiting to be released.

"Now imagine what you could do with the energy in each of these feathers," the Mother replies, her eyes gleaming. "Imagine the fury you could unleash."

With these little gifts Slater has given me.

I whisper a command to the feather to return to the satchel, after which the Mother reaches for my hands again.

"You are limited only by the boundaries you place around yourself," she says.

"Boundaries," I murmur, a sliver of self-doubt creeping back in. "If I now control the power of all three—the Maiden, the Mother, and the Crone—all at once, what does this mean for my vow of purity?"

A smile plays around the Mother's mouth. "You're wondering how a Maiden can also be a Crone?"

I give her a nod, fighting the burn in my cheeks.

"You carry the core attributes of all three," she replies. "As the Maiden, you draw on the power of your heart and compassion. That is where the power of the

Maiden truly lies. If it were your only power, you would need to do everything you could to maintain your purity to stay at your strongest. But you're not only the Maiden anymore."

Her smile grows and a twinkle enters her eyes. "The Crone's power is built on desire. Desire for dominance, vengeance, and pleasure. You will not destroy your Maiden power if you embrace this new side of yourself. In fact, your three powers will work in harmony, and you will only grow stronger."

I exhale slowly, sensing the lifting of a boundary I've placed around myself.

A moment later, the Crone appears on the path from the castle. She's juggling a mountain of objects, the outline of which becomes clearer as she approaches.

Boots. Another satchel. Various items of clothing.

"I've slowed time within our haven," she says, her voice a little muffled behind the items she's carrying. "It's now a fraction of the passage of time outside. An hour here is ten minutes out there."

She drops to her knees beside us. There's more color in her cheeks and her silver hair is swept back from her face, the strands gleaming once more. I consider her with a fresh outlook, appreciating the extent to which she must restrain her fundamental nature on a daily basis.

"I have a feeling I may have nothing more to teach you," she says to me with a quiet smile. "So I've brought you gifts to keep you safe."

She allows the pile of offerings to settle in her lap before she lifts them one at a time to show me what they are, then places them on the grass beside her. "Boots for Slater. I adjusted an old pair of my shoes so they would fit him. This satchel is to carry your potions—it's covered in a protection spell so that its contents won't smash if it's dropped or you're attacked. And these"—she shows me the bodice, pants, and second pair of boots she brought with her—"are battle clothes."

She hands those directly to me. "They're a set of mine that I wore long ago. I've adjusted them for your size and body shape."

I consider the clothing with gratitude.

Each item is black. The boots are knee-high and feel like they're made of the supplest material.

"Thank you," I say.

The Crone reaches into her pocket and slowly withdraws two smaller objects. "I also made these for you."

She holds out her hands so that I can see the pieces of black lace jewelry resting in them.

A new choker and bracelet.

"I've infused them with my power so you can draw on it if you need it."

I don't know what to say, swallowing hard against the lump in my throat.

Unable to speak, I reach up to the white choker around my neck. It breaks free at the slightest tug. Then I unclip the lace bracelet from the pearl ring and pull the lace off my wrist. It was already fraying and it disintegrates at the edges.

The pearl ring has turned completely black, so I leave it where it is.

I fold up the broken pieces of lace before I reach for the new black jewelry, accepting both pieces from the Crone before I press the old lace into her palm.

She closes her hand around the broken, white pieces. "I placed these on you when you were a toddler. They were spelled to grow as you grew. For protection and purity and hope." She gives me a smile that warms my heart. "But you don't need them anymore."

I lean forward and hug her, pressing my cheek to hers and accepting the dampness of her tears against my skin.

"Thank you for keeping me alive and safe all these years."

She gives me a teary nod. "I wish we could come with you. But we'll only be a liability."

I shake my head. "You need to stay here and watch over the fates of this world. There will undoubtedly be battles ahead for others in this world and darkness will threaten to rise. You must be here for all of it."

The Crone's attention turns to Slater as he approaches along the path. "I'm grateful that you won't be alone, Emmaline."

She swipes hurriedly at her wet cheeks and clears her throat before Slater reaches us.

Pasting a business-like smile on her face, she says, "I've created the passageway I promised you. It's in the inner wall of the glass atrium." She gestures back to the castle. "It will open at your approach and take you directly into the portal in the Sahara."

She rises back to her feet and the Mother follows her.

"We'll give you some privacy to get ready now," the Crone says. "Come to the castle when you're ready."

"And remember," the Mother adds with a smile, "Ethna has slowed time within our home. You don't need to hurry."

CHAPTER 28

EMMALINE

T he Mother and the Crone turn away before
Slater reaches me. He's nursing the potions he
gathered in the hem of his shirt.

"Everything okay?" he asks.

"As okay as it can be," I reply, placing the black lace
carefully on top of the fresh clothing before I take the
potions he offers and slip them into the satchel one
by one.

When I'm done, I reach for him, wrapping my arms
around his waist and pressing my head to his chest.

He draws me closer, his heart beating steadily at
my ear.

"I don't know what will happen," I whisper. "But I
know I want you with me."

In response, he presses a kiss to my temple and we
stay like that for a long moment.

Finally, I retrieve my new clothing and lead Slater to

the willow tree, where I slip between the fronds, taking him with me into the calm pocket behind them.

I turn to face him fully before I lift my white dress up over my head and drop it to the glistening ground. I remove my underpants and even, for now, the copper penny.

For the first time in a very long time, I'm completely naked.

When I don't make any move to dress myself, he steps closer.

The desire in his eyes heats me to my core. "Emmaline?"

"I'm not bound by my vow any longer." I step right up to him, pressing my palm to his heart before I reach up on tiptoes to place a soft kiss on his lips. A questioning kiss.

His arms sweep around me, and his fingers splay against my naked back. He groans against my mouth as he deepens the contact, allowing me to explore his lips.

I press closer, and even though my palm and my breasts are crushed between us, it feels like the distance between our bodies is too wide. A distance I need to close.

I pull back just enough to speak. "How do I ask for more?" I say. "How do I ask you for everything?"

"You just do," he replies, a low rumble of sound.

His gaze passes across my face like a caress and his hands slide slowly up and down my back, but he doesn't take it further, waiting for me to articulate what I want.

I nudge his lips with mine, tasting darkness and light, the warmth of the sun and the cold of night.

"I want everything," I whisper. "I want all of you."

The play of his fingers across my back makes me shiver as he lightens his touch. "I heard the Mother say we don't have to hurry. Is that correct?"

"Yes."

The heat in his eyes increases. "Then I don't plan to hurry." His lips brush mine, a touch as light as his hands, but his voice deepens with determination. "I don't know what the future holds, Emmaline, but I won't waste a second of the moments I have with you."

His lips cross to the corner of my mouth and then travel lower to my jaw, nudging against the side of my neck, across my earlobe, and down to the top of my shoulder, where he lingers. All the while, his hands continue to play across my skin, now sliding down my sides to my hips, where his thumbs brush my lower stomach.

I take my chance to reach for the hem of his shirt, tugging it upward. He leans back a little to remove it and drop it to the ground.

I'm already reaching for the button of his jeans. He watches me with a growing smile as I slip the button free and draw down the jean's zipper. I half-expect him to catch my hand before I can slip my palm against his hard length, but he seems happy to let me do as I please.

For a moment.

His eyes close briefly and a groan passes his lips, but as soon as I lean forward with my own moan of need, he clasps my hand and draws it away.

He steps back to remove his clothing.

The need to press my body against his is too intense for me to ignore.

I collide with him. Skin on skin.

He wraps me up in his arms, pulling me against him, lifting me up and guiding my legs around his hips—but too high to fit together this way.

In the next moment, he lowers me to the ground, my back against the soft grass, the lights in the tree twinkling down on us. His mouth closes over my left breast, his tongue teasing my nipple, but only lightly, before swirling across to the side, leaving the nub hard wanting as he continues down to my stomach.

He kisses my left hip and the top of my thigh, passes across my center, and then nudges the inside of my right thigh.

At the same time, his hands stroke my sides, reaching up to my breasts but resting against them, a stillness that drives my need to new heights. I take matters into my own hands, arching and pressing up against his palms, rocking against him in an attempt to ease the ache.

His mouth closes over my center at the same time I move and the sudden pleasure spiking through my body nearly makes me scream.

While his tongue continues to taste me, he works a finger slowly inside me. Then a second finger. His touch is shallow, leaving me wanting until, again, I take matters into my own hands and push against him, drawing his fingers deep inside.

It only makes me ache more badly.

"Slater," I finally gasp, losing my battle against the desperate need rising inside me. "Please fuck me."

I sense him smile against my center.

When he speaks, his voice is a vibration that hums against my clit. "I want your body to be ready."

"I'm ready now."

Again, he smiles, and the slow movement of his mouth against me drives me crazy. "*More* ready."

Readier than this? I rock against him as his tongue resumes its tantalizing swirls and his fingers move slowly in and out.

I clench around his hand, demanding more, and the pressure alone brings me to the brink of an orgasm.

He seems to sense it, pulling his hand away, easing up on my center at the same time, leaving me on the edge.

But not for long.

In the next instant, he rises up over me, slipping his arms behind my back and lifting me into a sitting position with him so that I'm straddling him. The desire in his eyes and the quickness of his breathing as his chest presses to mine tell me that he isn't as in control as I thought he was.

"If you want more, then you can have it," he says. "It's your choice."

My heart burns as I consider the freedom that he's giving me to make sure this is something I want to do.

But I already know it isn't a want. It's an undeniably wild *need*.

I lift myself a little, taking hold of his hard length at the same time, fitting the tip of his cock to my center. I'm slick with need and there's barely any resistance as I lower myself down, my muscles relaxed as I take him inside me until he's fully seated within me.

Deep pleasure sends my senses into a dizzying spin.

I press one hand against his heart and curl the other around his shoulder, trying to brace myself.

My breathing is barely in control as I rise up again, forcing myself to take it slow, every spike in pleasure nearly drowning me.

This time, I plunge downward. My body fits neatly around him, and the burst of sensations draws a cry to my lips.

He responds with a kiss, his lips warm against mine while his left hand closes around my hips and his right hand rests between us, his thumb pressing to my clit.

I take and give with every plunge, my movements becoming more unrestrained, letting go until I'm aware of him taking control.

He thrusts upward and I brace, crying out as the pleasure only intensifies, driving every other thought from my mind.

He is everything.

On the next thrust, I scream and shatter, the orgasm breaking me apart, tearing at my heart and soul, and mending me, all at the same time.

He comes hard, groaning my name and bucking against me as I continue to ride his body. His final thrust only drives the pleasure higher, another orgasm breaking across me, hot and intense.

I land back in his arms, my chest heaving while I

accept his kisses against my cheeks, wanting this moment to never end.

No matter what happens after this, I'm certain I won't wear white again.

CHAPTER 29

SLATER

I want nothing more than to wrap her up in my arms and stay within this quiet cavern surrounded by glimmering lights.

Her body is soft and her kisses are sweet, but the wild in her eyes hasn't disappeared. She's glowing with renewed power, and the streams of energy between us feel completely natural now.

Finally, we rise from the canopy floor, and I fight what's waiting for us once we leave this place.

I reach for the new black choker and ask her permission to place it around her neck.

When she nods and lifts her hair out of the way, all I have to do is lift the choker toward her throat and the magic takes hold, sealing the lace. When I wrap the lace bracelet around her wrist, it also seals magically, after which I clip the black chain at its base to her newly-darkened ring.

Then I place the penny back around her neck, the chain allowing it to nestle at the base of her choker.

She doesn't take her eyes off me, a soft smile on her lips as I pull on my clothing.

I dress her in the way that I want to *un*dress her, taking my time pulling on her black underwear, the black pants that fit her snugly, and finally the black leather bodice that hugs her curves.

Touching her drives my fears away.

When I step back, taking in her new ferocity, I'm reminded that I saw her like this. Out in the desert when she first appeared to me. I saw her dressed in all black leather, the heat of desire in her eyes.

Leaning forward until I'm a breath away from her lips, I say, "I'll make you a promise, Emmaline." I demand her gaze, searching her eyes for the wild determination she showed me when her magic protected me from Adeline. "I promise to give you everything you need, once we survive this."

Her focus drops to my lips but quickly returns to my eyes. "Then we should go now because I'm already impatient for more."

I can't stop the smile from breaking across my face.

Reality is pushing at me, but I refuse to allow this moment to darken because of the danger ahead of us.

I lace my fingers with hers before I lead her outside.

Then I pause again, contemplating the objects hanging from the Tree of Lost Things. "Should we take any of these with us?"

Emmaline studies several of them. "If I knew exactly

what awaited me, I might be able to judge that with more certainty. But there's a risk that I could take something I don't need, and it might fall into the wrong hands. I protect them here in the haven to prevent that exact scenario from happening."

She shakes her head as she seems to make up her mind. "I should leave them here."

"Okay, then."

We retrieve the two satchels along the way—the brown one that holds the feathers and the black one containing the potions.

I quickly pull on the boots.

When we reach the castle and step into the glass atrium, I can see a large circle of glittering magic on the left-hand wall. It glistens among the greenery as if it were painted across the leaves.

I heard the Crone say earlier that the passageway will open when we approach, so I keep my distance from it for now.

Emmaline hovers in the glass entrance for a moment, but her presence seems to be all that her sisters needed, appearing in a whirlwind of icy power that nearly knocks me off my feet.

At least this time, they're not trying to kill me.

They take one look at her before they hug her. Their expressions are drawn, but they each murmur to her in the ancient language and I translate their words as protection spells.

The Mother pulls away first, leaving Emmaline with

the Crone for another few moments as she makes her way to me.

She holds up a gleaming blade with a black handle, along with a harness to place around my waist.

"You are a mercenary, are you not?" she asks when I hesitate to take the weapon.

I give her a nod. I don't want to tell her that the only times I've killed, I've done so with my hands. Blades are messy—and can become liabilities—but I don't reject her gift since it's given with good intentions.

Taking the harness first, I strap it around my waist before I accept the dagger. "Thank you."

Emmaline and the Crone approach us quietly.

"Once you enter the passage, you will step straight into the center of the Saharan portal that leads to the old country," the Crone says. "You won't encounter the Portal Watch on our side of the portal, but if Adeline is waiting for you on the other side, she will see you coming. You must be prepared for an attack in those moments when you pass through."

"She needs our fight to be public," Emmaline replies. "But that won't stop her from trying to injure me to gain an advantage. I'll be ready."

So will I.

Emmaline is going up against a witch who has had years to prepare and has access to all number of powers. Even if Emmaline survives the fight with Adeline, she'll face Adeline's mother.

"The passageway will close as soon as you pass through it," the Crone continues. "It's built to be one-way only so that an attack can't be launched through it from the other side."

"That's okay," Emmaline says, glancing at me. "We'll find another way back."

Her sisters gather her into a final hug, and I take myself to the side—a little too close to the passageway. The glittering circle begins to burn more brightly, the vines and glass wall becoming transparent.

Colors from the other side start to show through.

Or rather, a lack of color.

The outline of a dark environment is slowly becoming visible.

I turn back to Emmaline as she steps up to my side.

Behind her, the Crone and the Mother are standing close to each other and, now that Emmaline's back is to them, I experience the full force of their fear and sadness. All of the emotion it seems they didn't want to show her.

I want to tell them that I'll bring her back safely.

"It feels as if time is rushing past me now," Emmaline whispers. "Pulling at me like the flow of a river that I've been swept up in. I'm tumbling along and there's nothing I can do to slow down."

She meets my eyes for a charged moment.

"Let's go," she says, staying at my side as we step together into the burning circle.

Our destination opens up in front of us.

The passageway disappears behind us and then we're standing in an open patch of ground in front of what might have once been a verdant forest.

Gray clouds boil above burned-out trunks and fallen branches. The ground is blackened. Covered in soot.

As much as the stark environment puts me on edge, our welcoming party is my greatest concern.

Adeline paces back and forth only a few steps away, her dark clothing matching our environment. Her red-streaked hair and blood-red eyebrows are a blaze of color against the dark backdrop.

A man stands beside her, and I quickly size him up. He's also dressed in black but carries what appears to be a sword at his back, judging by the hilt that's visible above his left shoulder. Which means he's right-handed. He's the same height as me, the visible part of his biceps and forearms heavily muscled.

He has a long scar down the left side of his face. It cuts close enough to his cheekbone that he's probably lucky he didn't lose his eye.

What really surprises me is the absence of visible power flowing from him to Adeline. If Adeline were tapping into his power, I should be able to see it, the same way that Emmaline and I can discern the shadowy flow of energy between us. The same way I could see the Mother's hidden bracelet and the Crone's true face beneath her glamour.

Yet there's nothing between these two.

The warlock's focus is on us in a flash.

At the same time, Adeline stops pacing. "You came."

"You sound surprised," Emmaline replies.

Adeline's gaze rakes over her. "You changed your

clothes." A flicker of wariness enters her expression. "The Maiden never wears black."

"Is that why you aren't wearing white?" Emmaline asks.

"I gave up the white years ago," Adeline snaps, striding forward.

At her approach, light bursts from Emmaline's hands, a protective shield gleaming around us.

Adeline pulls up sharply, her hands raised, palms visible. "Relax, Emmaline," she says. "Now that you're here, I intend to play fair."

She pauses before she gestures at our surroundings. "Just don't expect the same from my mother. After all, *this* was her idea of mercy."

I sense Emmaline's growing unease through the magic flowing between us. She doesn't lower the gleaming shield, but it becomes less bright. "This place carries the heaviness of death."

Adeline presses her lips together, continuing to appraise Emmaline before she sighs. "Intolerable, isn't it?"

Taking a step back, she inclines her head at the man beside her. "Jensen is loyal to me. He'll escort us to the palace, where you'll meet my mother. If you try anything before we reach our destination, you can expect to feel the sting of his power."

Electricity crackles around Jensen's hands as if to illustrate Adeline's speech. The energy within his power buzzes in my senses, warning me that he's strong.

He shuts it down, but the sparks leave bright spots in my vision.

Adeline points to the edge of the burned forest. "The passageway is over there. The sooner we get to the palace, the better. Follow me."

"Watch your step," Jensen snarls before he follows after Adeline.

I'm surprised that they're willing to turn their backs on us, but I should expect them to be confident in their power.

Judging by Emmaline's expression, it has unsettled her, too. "Be careful," she whispers. "I'll maintain the protective shield around us, but don't let down your guard."

I'm about to reply when I take my first step.

My boots crunch.

I glance down at the scorched earth.

I'm standing on bones.

CHAPTER 30

EMMALINE

Into the dark forest we go.

The path to the trees is lined with bones that crumble beneath my boots. Many of them seem to have been trodden on before, ground to white dust that lifts in the languid breeze.

It's only taken me a few steps to fully understand why my sisters never wanted me to come back here.

Already, my heart is hurting with all the pain that has bled into this earth. Beside me, Slater is tense, his jaw clenched, but in a way that reassures me he's ready to act if needed. I didn't miss the look in his eyes when we stepped onto the ashen ground littered with bones. Simmering anger fills his expression.

He knows what it's like to lose family to senseless acts of war.

Ahead of us, Adeline appears to be counting steps as she passes through the trees, whispering beneath her breath, finally slowing and stopping in front of a badly-burned trunk.

"It's this one," she says to Jensen before she presses her hand to the uppermost knot of bark.

Casting a quick glance back at us, she explains. "The entrance moves each time it's used."

At her touch, the tree trunk splits down the front, each side opening and grating against the ashen ground. A narrow staircase is revealed, into which Adeline steps.

Jensen gestures for us to go before him, and Slater moves behind me, making a barrier out of himself between me and the scarred man.

The steps descend into a similarly narrow—and very dark—tunnel. I'm tempted to test my new powers to create lamps along the way, but Adeline beats me to it.

She flings little fireballs left and right as she strides along the now-flat terrain, sending several ahead of us to light the way.

"This passageway is designed to get us to the palace quickly. The trip aboveground would take a day on foot, but we don't have that much time." Her dark-brown eyes flash at me. "It took months for the raven shifter to find you. My mother has grown impatient. And when she's impatient, she likes to take her bad temper out on others."

Slater's hand on the small of my back is a constant reassurance. So is the satchel of potions I'm carrying, as well as the bag of feathers he's transporting.

It was surprising to me that Adeline didn't attack me on sight, but even more so that she hasn't tried to take anything away from us, including the dagger that Slater is wearing in plain sight.

"Where exactly are we going?" I ask.

"I told you," she says, throwing her response back over her shoulder. "To the palace."

"To meet your mother."

"She wants to see you before you die," Adeline replies.

"You sound very confident that you'll beat me."

Adeline doesn't reply and with her back to me, it's impossible to tell what she's thinking.

"I thought there would be gatekeepers at the portal back there," I say.

Adeline snorts. "My mother doesn't need gatekeepers anymore. Anyone who steps through the portal from our side is burned to ash."

All that death...

"Even so, I'm surprised you met me at the portal with only one warlock as backup." I glance back at Jensen.

I'm fishing for information and I'm not sure if Adeline will take the bait. What I find curious is that she doesn't seem to be tapping into Jensen's power...

Adeline's reply is terse this time. "You expect me to reveal all my power sources at once? Did I not mention that my mother doesn't know what I've done? I don't exactly traipse around advertising the fact that I've acquired—"

The sound of running footfalls cuts her off.

I make out a small figure up ahead, their long, blonde

hair flying back and forth in the dark. The lightness of their footfalls indicates they could be a child.

Adeline darts forward. "Kaylee?"

I crane around Adeline to make out the girl's features. Drawn, pale, her cheeks tear-streaked. She can't be more than ten years old. One shoulder of her tattered dress is burned, her visible skin raw and bloody.

"Adeline!" she cries, racing toward us.

From behind Slater, Jensen pushes forward, plastering himself against the wall in the narrow pass so he can move ahead of Slater and me.

Once clear, he races forward, catching the girl before she would reach Adeline. "Kaylee! What happened?"

He drops to a crouch and Adeline squeezes in beside him, both of them checking Kaylee over.

Kaylee's breaths wheeze in and out of her mouth as she chokes back her sobs. "She took Rozanne."

"What?" Adeline's gasp is sharp, but Jensen's response is sharper.

"Fuck!" Wild shadows play across his face as his focus flies to Adeline. "I have to get to her. I can't let my sister suffer."

"Jensen, no!" Adeline grabs his arms, holding on tightly. "She wants to draw you in. She wants me to make a mistake. You have to trust me."

When he continues to pull away, she presses her palms to his cheeks, forcing him to look at her. "Trust me. Augusta won't do anything until I get there."

"You don't know that—"

"I do! Because it's the threat that matters. The fear.

The dread. That's what she feeds on. You know this. And you know I won't let her hurt Rozanne."

Jensen's jaw clenches. The tension in the air is unbearable. If the Queen feeds on fear and dread, then this tunnel contains a smorgasbord I'm sure she'd love.

Jensen doesn't appear to capitulate, his muscles remaining tense, but he doesn't immediately jump to his feet, either.

Adeline turns back to Kaylee, continuing to check over her wound as she asks, "Where is Rozanne now?"

"She's with the Queen," Kaylee says, wincing as Adeline lifts a flap of burned material away from her shoulder. "They're at the arena."

"Already?" Adeline lowers the material before she rubs her temples. "She wants to make sure I go through with it. She's using Rozanne as leverage to draw me straight to the arena. That way, I can't back out."

Adeline stares at the tunnel ahead. "This passageway lets out into the palace. It will take us too long to get from the palace to the arena. I don't want my mother getting irritated. We need another way to get there. Fast."

I speak up. "I can help you."

The moment I speak, Slater's hand tightens against my back.

Adeline glares at me. "Why would you help? The arena is where we'll fight. You'll only be hastening your own death."

I sigh. "Again, you assume you'll beat me. But yes, if your friend is in danger and I can help her, then I will."

"Fucking Maiden," Adeline whispers.

I let her anger wash over me. It's clear to me it comes from a place of fear. "I can help Kaylee, too, if you'll let me. I have a healing potion with me."

Again, Slater's hand presses against my back, and I understand his concern. I didn't bring an endless supply of potions and I may desperately need the healing ones for myself.

"I am who I am," I whisper, leaning back toward him.

He presses forward to meet my touch, his cheek briefly brushing mine. "Dammit, Emmaline."

But he doesn't try to stop me when I carefully slide my satchel onto the dusty tunnel floor and bend to it, keeping my movements slow. "I'm getting out a potion now," I say, more for Adeline's and Jensen's benefit, since they could suspect I'm about to remove a weapon.

They watch me carefully, eyes narrowed with suspicion as I move, but Kaylee's tear-filled face calms the longer she studies me.

"Raven," she murmurs.

I miss a beat since I'm not sure if she's talking about Slater or me. I guess it doesn't really matter. We're both here and we can both help.

I pull a vial of golden potion from the satchel and hold it out to Adeline. "This is a healing potion. Kaylee needs to drink it. It will mend the burn."

Adeline simply glares at me. "It could be poison."

"Hmm." I slip the lid off the vial and touch it to my lips, ensuring it's clear that I swallowed some. Then I offer it to her again. "It isn't poison."

She reaches across the small gap between us and snatches the potion from me, lifting it to Kaylee's lips.

The girl swallows it down in seconds, and moments later, the heavy furrow in her brow clears. Her burned skin starts to regenerate, smoothing over until the burn is completely gone.

Kaylee smiles back at me, but Adeline only stares, her lips compressed.

"You said you can help us get to the arena faster," she says. "Tell me how."

"I can open a portal. But you need to describe our destination to me."

"It's a large stadium. Circular," Adeline says. "Knowing my mother, the stands will be packed. Not because anyone wants to be there to watch your death. She will have made them attend."

"Okay, then." I take a deep breath. "Are you ready?"

She glares at me. "Are *you*?"

With a soft exhale, I twist to face the side of the tunnel as I draw on my power, taking a little energy from Slater this time.

But I pause before I release the force pooling in my hands. "We don't have to be enemies," I say to Adeline. "We both want the same thing."

Her brow furrows fiercely, and it's the only response she gives me.

Drawing my hands through the air, I firmly fix an image of the stadium in my mind. "*Give me passage to the witch's arena.*"

The sparkling circle that forms on the side of the tunnel lights up the space around us.

On the other side of it, a large, open stadium appears.

I hang back, waiting for Adeline to walk in first. I suspect that Jensen will bring up the rear to make sure I don't back out, so, with a brief glance at Slater, I step into the arena.

The soil beneath my feet is black like crumbled coal. The open space stretches about two hundred feet in each direction and the stands around it appear to be built from gray rock that might once have sparkled but is now dull.

Slater stays close at my back, and Jensen hurries through last, keeping Kaylee close.

The stands are packed with onlookers.

I expect to feel the instant energy of their witch and warlock powers, but only a weak haze hovers around them.

Their faces are gaunt, but their attention on me is instant. There's a sudden hush as I step through the portal, and then whispers start. "*Raven.*"

The murmurs stop just as quickly. Their attention returns to a spot on my right-hand side, not more than fifty paces away.

A woman lounges on a throne swathed in velvet. She has dark hair like Adeline's but hers is streaked with pink. Her eyes are also pink—most certainly a glamour—and so are her long fingernails, which she's running through the brown hair of a warlock who kneels at the side of the throne. He smirks up at her, clearly enjoying the attention.

Ten warlocks gather around her, some of them standing in a semi-circle behind the throne, others kneeling like the brown-haired man. One of them is massaging her shoulders. Another warlock, this one blond, is stroking her left thigh.

The haze of power around them is a dizzying mix of elemental powers. All of them appear completely at ease, their expressions snide. I can only assume they are the favored few.

What really angers me is that a teenage girl is suspended in midair in front of the throne. She's hanging upside down, dressed in jeans and a T-shirt that appears tucked in tightly enough that it isn't hanging down around her face. Her fingertips and hair brush the ground. Her eyes are closed. She's undoubtedly unconscious and the shallow rise and fall of her chest tells me she's barely holding on.

Jensen's harsh whisper confirms her identity. "Rozanne."

The Queen considers us with sharp eyes. "There you are. Finally."

Adeline strides ahead of me, stopping only five paces from the throne.

I stay farther back, not only because I want space to act, but because every inch of my skin crawls in the presence of Queen Augusta and her warlocks. Every beat of my heart is like a scream waiting to be released as I take in the unconscious girl, the gaunt faces of the people, and even the way that Jensen has hung back, keeping Kaylee behind him, as if he fears she'll be the Queen's next target.

Already, my power is building within my chest, but I hold on to it. I tell myself to wait.

To act rashly could endanger the people in this arena.

I can't see Adeline's expression now because her back is to me, but her head tips slightly toward Rozanne. "Mother. Do you have so little faith in me that you thought I needed an incentive?"

The Queen gives a shrug. "I was bored. You took too long."

Adeline's shoulders are tense as she crosses the distance and takes a knee in front of the throne. She bows her head to her mother. "I'm here now, and I did what you asked. I brought Raven."

Augusta leans toward her daughter with a cold smile. "Well, let's make sure she's the real Raven, shall we?"

She leans back and addresses the blond-haired warlock who was stroking her thigh. "Ancel, get me a closer look at our guests."

Ancel inclines his head at the Queen before he grins at me, making my blood run cold.

In the next instant, he appears directly in front of me.

Yet he has also remained exactly where he was before, kneeling at the Queen's side.

Two of him?

No, wait...

"Astral projection," I say, staring back at him, maintaining a deadpan expression despite his nearness. "How interesting."

Beside me, Slater has tensed, his hand flying to his dagger, but I press my palm to his side, urging him to be calm.

"Welcome, Raven. You look just like your mother." Ancel's voice makes the hairs on the back of my neck stand on end. Mostly because, over on the throne, the Queen's lips move as he speaks.

She's speaking through him.

Dear fates. I wonder if she has cursed him to obey her or if he willingly gives his power over to her like this. Either way, there's a new suspicion forming in my mind.

I don't think the Queen is the only one tapping into Ancel's power...

"You should enjoy your last breaths," the Queen says through Ancel. "If my daughter fails to kill you, I will finish the job. For too long, you have been a sword hanging over my head. This ends today."

"It *will* end today," I reply quietly. "One way or another."

Ancel gives me a cold smile and this time, I suspect it's his smile and not the Queen's.

His projection disappears, snapping back to his body, leaving a mere streak of energy in his wake.

Keeping a calm demeanor, I rapidly reassess the other warlocks, identifying their powers based on the energy flowing around them.

Sunlight, frost, fire... And astral projection...

Those are all powers that I sensed Adeline was controlling when she broke through the haven's defenses.

Well. She isn't draining Jensen like I thought she

might have been. She's draining her mother's own warlocks.

It's a dangerous game for Adeline to play. The risk of her mother finding out is high. But it confirms for me what I felt in my heart: Adeline isn't my enemy. I'm not here to end her.

I'm here for her mother.

Adeline has remained bowed in front of the Queen, who leans toward her once more.

"Good girl. You did what I asked." The Queen pats Adeline on the head, but on the final pat, her fingers claw and she digs her long, pink fingernails into Adeline's scalp.

Adeline gasps, and I flinch to see blood appear between the strands of her hair.

The Queen's voice lowers to a harsh whisper. "And now you will kill her for me, or I will hurt everyone you care about. Starting with Rozanne."

Anger rises within me, but I'm not surprised by the ferocity of the emotion this time, and I don't try to push it away.

"Slater," I whisper, a harsh sound between my gritted teeth, "be ready."

It's time to embrace everything that I am.

CHAPTER 31
SLATER

"Enough!" Emmaline's voice takes on strength as she strides toward the Queen. "My fight is not with Adeline. It's with *you*!"

White light bursts from Emmaline's fist, striking the Queen's hand where she holds Adeline.

The Queen jolts backward, releasing Adeline from her clawed grip.

Adeline ducks and rolls, slipping away from her mother within seconds while the Queen gives a shriek of rage.

A rapid second blast of white light streaks from Emmaline's fist and pulses over Rozanne where she hangs in the air. I immediately recognize Emmaline's protective power flowing across Rozanne and I sense the break in the power that was keeping Rozanne suspended.

"Slater!" Emmaline cries. "Get Rozanne!"

I'm flying within seconds, swooping toward the unconscious girl. I pluck her out of the air before she can

263

fall, zooming upward to avoid the sudden strikes of power from the warlocks, who are now mobilizing behind the Queen.

Magic sizzles past me as I maneuver in the air, avoiding their attacks and speeding toward Jensen.

I drop to the ground and deposit his sister into his waiting arms, speaking quickly. "Take your sister and Kaylee to safety. Use the potions if you need them. Gold is for healing, red is for pain relief, lavender is for energy."

"Thank you. I'll use only what Rozanne needs." Jensen gives me a nod, before his focus flashes across both Adeline and Emmaline. "I'll keep the rest safe."

I don't have time for more.

Spinning back to Emmaline, my heart leaps into my throat.

She has risen into the air, levitating without wings, although I feel the pull of her power on my raven, and I sense the dark beauty in the way that Emmaline floats.

The Queen stands in front of her throne now, her warlocks clustered around her, each one of them gleaming with power that they're preparing to release.

A fucking rainbow of death that's about to rage toward Emmaline.

"Make your choice, Adeline!" Emmaline cries. "Fight beside me or against me."

Adeline is backing toward Emmaline. Blood trickles down her forehead from the cuts in her scalp, but I catch her smile as she turns her face up to Emmaline. "I already chose you."

"Okay, then." Shadows grow around Emmaline's body, hugging her curves while her hair floats around her head.

Movement catches my eye and I take my eye off her for a heartbeat to see the black feathers rise up out of the satchel, a swarm of them. They gather around Emmaline's body, forming the shape of burning wings at her sides.

When my feathers turned white, it felt like I was losing them.

Now, they feel found.

Quieter than the crackle of growing magic within the arena, I pick up the soft hum of whispers among the onlookers.

"*Raven.*"

That word is repeated over and over as the people in the stands lean forward. The hope in their eyes is painful to see, but I won't shy away from it.

No matter what it takes, I will protect Emmaline today. I fly closer to her, keeping enough distance between us that she won't be worried about hurting me when she makes her move.

In front of the throne, the Queen snarls at her warlocks. "Kill them." Her bright, pink eyes blaze at Adeline. "But make sure my daughter screams when she dies."

The warlocks fan out, prowling to the sides, their power forming growing streams of light.

The tension within the arena builds as I draw my

dagger, ready to fly among the warlocks and deal whatever death is needed.

I take another breath and then, in the space of a heartbeat, the stadium explodes with power, an instant and terrifying storm. Every kind of elemental power streaks toward Emmaline—

And then stops, rebounding off the transparent shield she placed around herself.

Explosion after explosion hits the shield, but it doesn't break. The warlock with astral powers—Ancel—tries to break through it, but his projection merely hits the barrier and disintegrates in a flash of light.

I stay where I am, ready to fight when Emmaline needs me.

Meanwhile, Adeline drops to a crouch, and I catch her whispers. An ancient spell that makes my blood run cold because it tugs at the curse within me. Except that I have no doubt it's not aimed at me.

Ancel suddenly roars, a sound of pain, as he drops to the ground clutching his heart.

Opposite him, Adeline's arm is outstretched, her hand turning in the air as if she has reached into his chest and is twisting his heart.

In the next moment, her other hand flies forward, and every one of the warlocks drops to the ground with a roar of pain.

The Queen whirls from one to the other. "Stop her! Stop my daughter!"

The warlocks writhe on the ground and, with every

passing second, power grows around Adeline's body—
their powers—building in strength.

"*Stop her!*" the Queen screams again.

She raises her hands and dark power shoots from her
fist, colliding with Emmaline's shield, which now encom-
passes Adeline, too.

The Queen's dark power sizzles and fades against the
force of the barrier.

Adeline slowly rises into the air, levitating beside
Emmaline, power streaking around her body like a tornado.

"Your reign is over, Mother," Adeline says.

The Queen raises her hands, dark light growing
again. "You won't defeat me. But when you discover how
pitiful your power is against me, know this: I will not
show you mercy. I will kill everyone you love—"

"Enough." Emmaline's quiet whisper is drowned in
the Queen's shrieked threats, but I hear it as clearly as if
Emmaline was standing beside me.

She and Adeline exchange a glance and, in unison,
they release their power.

The storm of warlocks' energy rages toward the
Queen from Adeline's hands.

The black feathers that Emmaline controls are swept
up in it, each one glowing as brightly as a firestorm.

The Queen's eyes widen a second before the storm
hits her.

The explosion of power tears my senses apart, a blast
of energy that obscures the Queen and the dying
warlocks. It radiates outward, lighting up Emmaline's

silhouette and then Adeline's as they brace against the force.

I can't breathe, but it doesn't matter. All that matters is that they succeed in ending the Queen.

My instincts buzz.

The hair on the back of my neck stands on end. And in the next moment, I watch the power that was rushing outward pull back in like an explosion in reverse.

An implosion of energy, sucking back toward the Queen.

Her silhouette reappears, completely unharmed. Her arms are outstretched as she pulls the power inward, gathering it into her arms and taking control of it.

Her laughter is jarring. "Thank you for giving me all of this power," she jeers. "Enough to destroy you both."

My heart is leaping into my throat, but my reflexes have already kicked in.

Emmaline!

I don't have time to call her name.

She's throwing herself toward Adeline and her protective power is thickening, but I'm not sure if it will be enough. *How can it possibly be enough?*

I'm a heartbeat away, ready to wrap my wings around them both and turn myself into another layer of protection when the Queen releases her gathered power.

It explodes across my back just as I collide with Emmaline in the air.

Burning flames, freezing ice, the numbing weight of stone. Pain beyond anything I've ever felt tears through me. The impact knocks us through the air and rips Emmaline out of my arms.

In the background, I'm aware of the people screaming in the stands and ducking for cover.

Emmaline and Adeline hit the ground, rolling across the dusty coals, smoke rising from their bodies. The jagged ground rips through my wings, tearing at my feathers as I skid across the earth. My white feathers spark at the impact, power rising off them, but the pain I'm feeling now... It tells me that I'm alive.

Farthest away from me, Adeline appears to be breathing, but her eyes are closed.

Closer to me, Emmaline's chest is rising and falling steadily where she lies, facing upward. Her eyes are open, but she isn't otherwise moving.

"Emmaline!" My exclamation comes out as a faint groan.

I give a mental roar at my legs and arms to *move*, forcing myself to crawl toward her, only making it a few feet before a shadow falls over me.

The Queen looms above me, peering down, her lips twisted with apparent disgust, before she turns her attention to Emmaline.

She kneels beside her, flicking Emmaline's hair away from her face. "You thought you could end me, didn't you?" She tuts at her. "I've spent years building up my resistance to all forms of magic. Not to mention, my daughter's attempt to drain my warlocks' power is nothing compared to the power source I control."

She lifts her hands, gesturing from side to side at the crowd. "Behold, *my* power source."

My gaze flies across the crowd, all the hundreds of energy sources that the Queen claims to be tapping into to keep herself alive.

It's too many.

Emmaline gives a groan and her hands twitch. Her gaze turns to me. There's a dangerously intense light in her eyes now, a burning flame that hasn't extinguished, and my instincts flare again.

What is she trying to tell me?

I replay the explosion in my mind, and then my eyes widen.

Emmaline used the feathers, but she didn't use her own power.

She created a protective shield, but that was all.

She barely scratched the surface of what she can do.

"Take my energy." I groan, daring to speak aloud, even though the Queen can hear me.

Emmaline's smile is soft but certain. "Never. I have enough power within myself and, if I need to, I'll give everything I have."

Alarm rises within me. "No—"

The Queen is taking incredulous glances between us, her brow furrowed with apparent displeasure. "Did you not hear me?" Her voice rises. "No magic can defeat me."

"I believe you," Emmaline says, looking up at her. "But I wonder how you'll fare against a blade."

The Queen's brow furrows.

I sense Emmaline's power like an ocean wave rolling in. Or maybe the sun coming out. Possibly both.

It's warm like her heart. Peaceful like her hopes. Strong like her will. Burning like the *wild* within her.

She closes her eyes, and a tear rolls down her cheek.

There's a *crack*. My heart feels like it's ripping apart. And then her power explodes from her chest.

It rushes outward, a wash of white, coating everything in its path, everything around us, in brilliant *glistening* magic. The coal dust we're lying on suddenly looks like powdered diamonds. The gray stone surrounding the arena takes on the appearance of white marble. Energy rushes through me. My wings are darker and brighter, both at once.

As Emmaline's power washes farther outward into the stands, every person begins to gleam, all of the colors of their skin and clothing suddenly vibrant.

Across the way, Adeline gives a groan and stirs, her red-streaked hair brilliant against the gleaming earth.

Everyone is glowing... but not the Queen.

She scoffs. "Very pretty, Raven," she says to Emmaline. "But also incredibly pathetic."

Emmaline arches her eyebrows, speaking quietly. "Is it?"

The Queen snorts, lowering her hand to Emmaline's heart, as if she's about to deal a killing blow.

Nothing more than a faint spark of light rises from her clenched fingers, a sputtering force.

She stares at her fist. Opens it. Closes it again. "My power..."

Emmaline smiles up at her. "My people are not your power source anymore. And they never will be again. I've protected them." She coughs, a slightly strained sound. "I've protected all of them."

The Queen jolts backward. "No."

Emmaline hasn't moved from where she lies, her voice remaining incredibly soft. "You said that I was a sword hanging over your neck. I think you must have known that fate would come for you in the form of a blade."

As she speaks, I tuck my wings and rise to a crouch, my focus suddenly clear. My feathers are ragged and my breathing labored, but I know what Emmaline wants me to do.

"What blade?" the Queen snarls.

My footfalls are quiet—as quiet as I've trained myself to be, a mere shadow, except that this time, I'm moving in the light.

"This blade," I say, sweeping my wings around the Queen.

She tries to turn, but my aim is swift.

The blow to her heart is direct and its effect nearly instant. Without her magic, she has nothing to fight back with.

She exhales one last time and her pink eyes turn to a dull brown as she slumps in my arms, and I lower her to the ground, leaving the dagger where it is in her chest.

When I rise back up, the arena is quiet.

Too quiet.

I spin to Emmaline, only to find Adeline leaning over

her, her hands swilling helplessly in the space above Emmaline's chest. "She isn't breathing..." Adeline looks up at me, tears flowing down her cheeks. "Emmaline isn't breathing!"

No...

I drop to my knees beside Emmaline. My chest is burning, my heart is tearing apart. The pain ripping through me is a destructive force. "She gave too much."

I'm reaching for her, gathering her still body up into my arms. I might be shouting, roaring out this pain in my chest, but I can't register anything except the fact that I could have stopped this.

She could have taken my life instead of giving hers.

Before I can wrap my wings fully around her, someone brushes my arm, and a little voice says, "Raven?"

I raise my eyes to find Kaylee beside me and at first, I think she's trying to address Emmaline, but she looks directly at me as she repeats, "Raven. Here."

In her hand is the second of Emmaline's golden potions.

Quickly taking it, I lift it to Emmaline's lips, my hands shaking so hard, I'm afraid I'll spill the liquid. Supporting her head, I pour it carefully past her lips.

Then I gather her back into my arms, pull her close again, and will her to hear me. "When you rescued me in the desert," I say, my voice nearly choking, "there you were, all dressed in white, glowing beneath the burning sun, but I saw double. Another you, dressed in black, your dark eyes daring me to give you my heart and soul."

I brush her cheek. "I give you my heart and soul, Emmaline."

I close my eyes, resting my forehead against hers.

Waiting. Hoping.

"I give you mine," she whispers back.

My eyes fly open.

Her eyelashes flutter against her cheeks, reminding me of the first time she woke in my arms.

"I give you my heart, Slater." Her eyes open fully, and her smile is more powerful than any she's ever given me.

Around us, the onlookers are rising to their feet, all of Emmaline's people covered in light, their eyes shining.

Adeline leans across us, her hand pressing to her heart before she says to Emmaline, "Welcome to your Queendom."

CHAPTER 32
EMMALINE
ONE MONTH LATER

I wake to soft kisses pressed against my bare shoulder blades.

Slater's hands graze down my sides, coaxing me awake. "Morning, mate."

I give a satisfied sigh as I turn in his arms, luxuriating in the kisses he trails down my chest and the instant heat they ignite within my core.

I open my eyes to gentle sunlight—the soft glow of my sisters' haven on Earth.

It's the first time I've returned here since I left for the old country and, even though this trip will be short, it's also the first time I've allowed myself to completely relax in weeks.

The last month in the old country is a blur. There's so much to be done to heal the people and the land. A world needs to be rebuilt from the ground up, and with Adeline and Slater at my side, I've made a start, but there's still a lot of work ahead of me.

A few days after the battle at the arena, Slater came back through the portal in the Sahara so he could return to his House and inform his king about everything that had happened.

The Mother and the Crone met us at the portal to give him quick passage back to the Gold and Garnet headquarters. I'd messaged them after the battle to let them know that I was safe and well, but it was the first time that I'd seen them after the battle and there were tears and hugs.

I had to fight my instincts to go with Slater to meet with his leader, Kaspian, but he said he needed to deal with it on his own.

I understood what he *wasn't* saying.

My power has grown exponentially, and I need to be careful that I don't upset the balance between Houses or threaten any House leader with my presence.

When Slater met with Kaspian, he requested permission to leave his House and be allowed to live with me in the old country. Kaspian agreed to the request on the condition that if he ever needed Slater—*really* needed him—Slater would answer the call for help.

As far as my own House is concerned, the Mother and the Crone simply told Odin and Lady Gabriella that I wasn't returning. I wasn't present for that encounter, but apparently, all Odin really wanted to know was whether or not war had been averted. When the Mother and the Crone told him that peace between the two worlds had been restored, he was satisfied with that.

He wished me well, but again, the subtext was that I

should stay in the old country and tread very carefully should I return to this world.

As for my sisters, they will need to find a new Maiden now so they can re-form a coven of three, but I know they will always welcome me here.

Here, in the haven, my presence is hidden, and I allow myself to let go of the weight of responsibility resting on my shoulders and enjoy my newfound freedom.

I moan against Slater's lips when he returns to my mouth.

"I want more," I murmur to him.

His lips rise into a smile that makes my heart beat faster. Sliding his arms beneath me, he rolls us over so that I'm on top, straddling him.

"Then take what you want," he says with a wicked smile, his hands resting lightly on the small of my back and his smoky eyes inviting me to take my pleasure from his body.

The first time with this man broke me and put me back together. Every time since then has felt like crashing, only to land in arms that will always catch me.

This time is no different. Every kiss, every stroke, every wild plunge has me crying out until we crash again.

And then again.

I'm boneless by the time he's kissed, explored, and stroked every part of my body, after which I fall asleep. Only to wake to kisses once more.

Every minute with Slater is time I will hold on to because I don't know what the future holds.

All I know for certain is that this is just the beginning for us.

We are mates, fated to be together.

We have a world to rebuild together, a life to share, and maybe, one day, a family to create.

Finally, I force myself from my bed, catching Slater's hand in mine and kissing him as we rise.

Before we return to the old country, there's one more thing I need to do.

It's time to return the penny to its owner.

No Man's Circus is every bit as dazzling as I suspected it would be—even if I can sense the pain its performers are concealing.

A bright spotlight shines on the blonde-haired woman spinning from a lyra in the center of the ring.

She's graceful, beautiful. *Broken.*

Even from a distance, I can feel the force of the memories she's folded up and put away inside her heart.

Her name is Liv and she's the penny's rightful owner. It took me an hour studying the tapestry of fates to discover her thread and her true identity. I wish that the Mother could have found her sooner, but it took the unique combination of my Maiden and Mother power to identify her thread.

The strand started off bright and full of hope but became thin and stretched.

Now, I'm determined to return the penny to her and

nudge her fate in the direction of hope again, even if finding the chance to speak with her will prove difficult.

The Ringmaster stands in the shadows at the side of the ring. He hasn't taken his eyes off Liv. His expression is closed off, but I read every small shift in the way his jaw clenches and how the tension around his eyes increases. He's taller than average—probably taller than Slater—and his muscular physique is clear even from a distance.

So is the fact that he's concealing his true power.

He is to be feared.

But not by me.

As if the man senses my gaze, his focus flashes to the stands, where Slater and I sit among the onlookers.

As he scans the crowd, a slight crease forms in his forehead.

He won't be able to single us out from the other patrons. Not yet, anyway. I've placed a light protection spell over us to conceal our true identities and a stronger spell to mask the strength of my power.

It's necessary to keep my strength concealed everywhere I go in this world. Now that I've come into my power, I could threaten the House leaders and I have no wish to do that. I've survived enough wars. I won't be the cause of another one.

The performance in the ring is nearing its end.

I unclasp the chain from around my neck and hold the penny tightly before I lean in to Slater, who is sitting on my left. "Stay close."

"Always."

Slater's focus is already on the Ringmaster. I trust Slater to watch my back, but also to make sure nothing harms Liv. I want to return her property to her, not put her life in peril.

As the show ends and the onlookers rise to their feet around us, I turn to the right—toward the performer's exit. It's the opposite direction to which the crowd is headed.

Casting a small and inconspicuous spell ahead of me, I cause the lingering patrons to step out of my way. They won't even realize why they're doing it. It clears my path so I can glide right over to the barrier at the side of the stands, at ground level with the performer's exit.

Liv is already striding along the path, and I almost miss my chance.

"Liv!" I use a trickle of my power to carry my voice to her, and to her alone. I would not betray her identity to anyone else.

Of course, she may not realize that.

She stiffens and slowly turns. I catch the flash of fear in her eyes before she conceals it, revealing nothing of the impact I've had on her by calling her name.

But I sense her feelings.

She doesn't trust me, and why should she? We aren't carrying visible weapons, and neither of us is dressed in anything unusual—jeans and T-shirts, all black in my case, although my choker may be slightly eye-catching. But appearances mean nothing to someone who will have learned never to trust anyone.

I sense her pulling away, so I act quickly, opening my

hand and allowing the copper penny to dangle from my fingertips.

Her eyes widen. For a painful second, the light of hope flares in her eyes and she edges forward, but then her focus flies to the Ringmaster.

He's watching her just as carefully now as he was when she was performing, but so far, he hasn't moved toward us.

She closes the gap between us, but she doesn't take the penny even when I hold it out to her.

It breaks my heart that her survival instincts are so deeply ingrained that she won't risk reaching for this object, which clearly means something to her.

"Where did you find that?" she asks.

We don't have time for long stories, so I give her a smile and hope it will suffice. "It belongs to you, does it not?"

I *will* her to take it, but when she continues to hesitate, I consider the Ringmaster again. My voice hardens a little. "Just as you currently belong to him."

The Ringmaster's glare is growing darker. He may not have been able to single us out before, but we've put ourselves in his path now—simply by speaking with Liv.

Slater brushes my arm, a warning signal. He edges farther to my left to block the Ringmaster's line of sight to me. If it weren't for the barrier at the side of the walkway, I'm sure he would step between Liv and the Ringmaster, too, and *damn*, I love that he would protect her if he could.

I lean toward Liv as she returns her attention to me,

wanting her to believe that she hasn't lost everything. That her freedom isn't entirely gone. That she can have it again.

"Don't be afraid," I whisper, keeping my voice as soft as possible as I continue to hold the penny out to her, urging her to reach out for it. "Take back what you lost."

Take back your life.

I hold my breath for the beat it takes her to close her hand around the penny.

A soft exhalation of relief passes my lips when she holds it close.

Finally, I've returned this powerful object to its rightful owner.

But I don't have time for more. We need to leave. Already, we've drawn the Ringmaster's attention and he's approaching us across the ring.

I won't allow my presence to worsen Liv's situation.

I slip my hand around Slater's arm and quickly, we turn away, preparing to disappear into the crowd.

Liv's soft voice calls out behind me. "Who are you?"

I take a beat. *Who am I?*

I'm the Maiden, the Mother, and the Crone. A vessel of purity, a reader of fates, and a dealer of vengeance. Raised by two witches who taught me to be strong and kind.

I'm Slater's mate. Queen of the old country.

A lost raven.

But more simply...

I glance back at her. "I'm Emmaline."

With a final smile, I step close to Slater's side, and we disappear into the crowd.

The End

⟡ ⟡ ⟡

If you'd like to check out the next standalone in this world, **Slay Me**, keeping reading for the first chapter!

Turn the page for the first chapter of Slay Me!

SLAY ME EXCERPT
BY JESSICA WAYNE

A bright spotlight shines down upon me, following my every step as I make my way into the center of the ring. The mat is soft beneath my bare feet, though the metal plates of my costume jingle as I move, a soft windchime-like noise that lulls the silent crowd filling the stands.

They're here to watch us perform. To feel something. Which is ironic given that the majority of us here at No Man's Circus no longer possess the emotional capacity required to feel anything more than hatred for the Ringmaster.

My gaze drifts across the space to a man wearing a red coat and black top hat. He stands at the edge of the ring, copper eyes on me. He's always watching. Staring. The others believe he waits for us to make a mistake so he can punish us.

I think it's more than that. What? I'm not sure. I've spent the last twelve years trying to figure it out because

I'm certainly not stupid enough to ask. Not even when we're alone. Knowing he's an unnecessary distraction, I turn my attention back to my performance.

Screwing up is not an option at No Man's Circus because our leader has killed for far less.

My hand closes on the steel ring suspended above me. I move in a circle, taking calculated steps as I await the music. One beat. Two. And then—the melody starts off like a lullaby, building just like a budding romance, so I slowly spin myself, taking the ring with me.

Still clinging to it, I'm lifted slowly until I'm suspended well above the ground. Up here, I lose myself in the sound, in the performance, because I can pretend that my world is far more than the gilded cage that is my reality.

I lift a leg and loop it through the lyra then pull myself up. With one leg dangling through the air, I continue to spin, arching my back to show off the skin revealed by a costume that portrays me as a goddess of war.

Of heartbreak.

Fitting, I suppose, given my past. Honestly, sometimes I wonder if the Ringmaster knows more about me than he lets on.

Magic sizzles along my skin, a dance of sparks thanks to the witch standing on a balcony hidden beneath the lights. Below, the crowd gasps and claps in delight while I continue to dance. They're watching, but all I can feel are *his* eyes on me.

Eyes that I long to look into even as self-preservation

tells me it's a horrible idea.

I drop down, letting one leg remain through the hoop, one hand on it. The lyra spins to the beat of the music, thanks to what little magic I do have. The breeze created by my power gently pushes strands of my near-white hair from my face.

As the tempo increases, so do my moves. Faster, faster, more erratic. If I had any feeling at all, I would ache for the woman in the song. A woman who lost everything because she chose to love the wrong man.

Right on cue, I release the ring.

And plummet.

The crowd gasps. Someone cries out below. But I'm not worried.

One more heartbeat and the firm body of my partner is beneath me. The griffin's feathers are soft beneath the flesh left exposed by my costume as I remain draped over his back, playing the part of a damsel. The crowd cheers as he brings me to the ground and lands before taking off again, disappearing into the shadows.

I wait, lying on the ground. My breathing is shallow, the entire ring suspended in complete silence as I lie. Even with my eyes closed, I can sense the Ringmaster. It makes no sense, of course. Although, seeing as how I have a penchant for attracting danger, I've come to consider it an additional sense. Some have great hearing, some sight. I *know* when someone possesses the ability to break me.

My heart pounds as a man kneels beside me. Even

though I'm unable to see him, I know it's my griffin—now shifted into the handsome man he is—pulling my limp body into his arms.

The music continues to play, building a faster beat as he strokes the side of my face. I open my eyes and look up into his yellow gaze.

Our performance is one of love. Of passion. And it's those emotions we try to elicit from our viewers. Something we're damn good at even if the very idea of a man putting his hands on me is something I can only tolerate while in this ring.

Golden hair falls to Apollo's broad shoulders. His muscled arms gather me closer, and he holds me against his strong chest for a brief moment. Then, the lyra is lowered again, and he reaches up to grab it. I wrap my arms around him, and he pulls me to my feet as the lyra is lifted.

He releases it, massive hands going to my hips as he presses my back to his front. I loop an arm around his neck, and we sway softly as the tempo slows once more.

The movements are all second nature to me now. But I still focus, unwilling to give a subpar performance because this is my freedom. Here, in this ring, I feel special in a world that has deemed me ordinary.

His hands drop, and I pull away, spinning around behind him until I'm right beside the lyra. I climb in, sitting on the steel like a swing, and my partner grips it with his hands as it flies into the air, disappearing from view.

The crowd's cheers are almost deafening as the lyra is moved toward the balcony where the witch waits for us.

"Great show, guys," Uma greets. Her black hair is in a braided crown above her head, the black cloak she wears adorned with shimmery stars and moons. She's as kind as she is gorgeous and is one of the few people here I trust to not stab me in the back.

I pull down the half-skull mask I wear over my nose and mouth to take a deep, uninhibited breath. "Thanks."

"You are always magnificent, Liv," Apollo offers. His charming smile would have been disarming if I weren't distrusting of anyone with a pulse. His tanned skin is stretched taut over solid muscle, making him a delectable sight to behold, nonetheless. A true hero in the eyes of all who see him.

All but me. Because I don't believe in heroes. Villains? Abso-fucking-lutely. They're all I believe in.

"You, too." I clap my hands together. "I am desperate for a drink."

Uma moves out of the way, remaining where she is to help with the next show. Apollo, however, follows me down the metal balcony and toward stairs leading to the performer-only section of the tent.

Bright lights shine above as everyone hustles around. Some prepare for their upcoming shows. Others are putting items away and getting ready for the final bow. The moment I think it, my stomach churns. It's the closest I ever am to the Ringmaster.

Even in private, he keeps his distance. Only watching me from his desk.

"Water?" Apollo hands me a cup.

I take it with a smile then drink the cool liquid. But as usual, it doesn't touch the heat burning inside of me. His hand goes to my lower back, and I inwardly cringe as I allow him to guide me over to a rundown couch in the corner. I don't mind being touched during our performance, but here in private, it feels more intimate.

Personal.

Using a drink to mask my hesitation, I let him take his seat first before joining him. Otherwise, he'll end up so close our thighs will be brushing. And, well, I have no intention of allowing him to think there is ever a chance of us engaging in anything more than what happens in that ring.

Still, he slings an arm over the back of the couch, the tips of his fingers grazing my bare shoulder. I fight a shiver, not wanting to cause conflict with the creature I hope will one day fly me the hell out of this place for good. Leaving without help—that's just not going to happen. Even if I escape the Ringmaster, Ernesto's men are still looking for me. Waiting for any opportunity to grab me. This time for good.

So, I play nice. Biding my time until I trust him enough to ask him to flee. Asking him sooner than that will be a death sentence.

"Felt good to be out there today. Even after what happened with Pima."

I grunt in agreement, the images of our murdered friend too much to deal with. Not that he's the first who's tried to run. It's always the same outcome. The Ringmaster's security detail drags them back in, and the three lion shifters make an example out of the one who attempted to run.

You get no second chances. No do-overs. One weak moment and you pay for it with your life. After all, that is what we signed over when the Ringmaster brought us in. At least, those of us who were lucky enough to have even half a choice.

Apollo was sold to the Ringmaster by his old house leader. While I never met Mathis, the griffin has told us all plenty about the shifter who ran Fire and Fluorite. How his selfishness was only outweighed by his brutality.

Once word of his death reached us here, I'm fairly certain Apollo expected someone to show up and barter for his release. When that day didn't come, he grew more agitated until two months ago when a fight with the Ringmaster nearly led to his death.

He'd been barely breathing by the time I found him.

Would have been dead had I not.

All because he questioned the Ringmaster.

"I'd get your arm away from the favored pet," Valentina all but sings. Her sparkly pink wings flutter quickly behind her as she floats above the floor. The pixie despises me, something she has never tried to hide. She's been here longer than me and, from what I understand, was in the process of seeking favor with the Ringmaster so she could buy her freedom back with the one thing she has to offer: her body.

When I was brought in, though, that changed. The

private performances began, and the pixie was pushed aside. Honestly, I'm fairly certain she spent the first year I was here trying to kill me. After all, one can only have their lyra fall from its suspensions so many times in the first week before suspicions are raised.

"Shut the fuck up, Val," Apollo snaps back at her.

"Fuck off," she replies, sticking her middle finger up in the air.

"Is that an invitation?" he asks. "Because I have to warn you, my beast does not take kindly to prissy bitches. I'll fucking ruin you."

"Funny since you are one," she replies sweetly.

Shaking my head, I tune them out and close my eyes. The constant bickering is too much to deal with, especially when I know there is so much worse out there. Creatures far more terrifying than the man who runs this twisted-ass circus.

"Get your thong out of your ass crack, Val."

I open my eyes as Fiona drops onto the chair across from me. Her ice blue eyes level on the pixie. White hair braided away from her face, she looks nothing like the savage I know she is. One of the only known female berserkers, she's rare. Important. And a hell of a lot stronger than anyone here.

Well, almost anyone. The Ringmaster takes the cake on that one. None of us knows how she actually came to belong to him, and it's not a story she will tell. My guess is it's similar to mine. She was cast out for being different.

"Stay the hell out of it, animal," Valentina quips.

Fiona grins at her. "Keep pushing on me, and I'll rip your wings off."

The pixie rolls her eyes but glides away quickly. *Smart move.*

"Great show tonight." Fiona pulls a blade off of her hip and begins to cut slices from a green apple. She pops them into her mouth and chews, the crunching sound making my stomach rumble. When was the last time I ate?

I'm fairly certain I had breakfast. But not lunch, right?

"Incoming," Fiona whispers as heavy footsteps echo in my mind.

The hair on the back of my neck stands on end and a shiver runs up my spine, ghostly fingertips that elicit far more heat within me than there should be.

Unwanted as it is, I've still come to expect this response to the man who pulled me from that alley a dozen years ago. The Ringmaster makes his way into the room, commanding a presence without ordering one. His copper eyes find me almost instantly, and a low growl leaves his lips. "I hate to interrupt your nap," he growls. "But your job is not over."

"We're just catching our breath before the final performance," Apollo replies.

The Ringmaster takes a step closer, and I sit up, fear spurring my movements. "We were just getting up to prepare," I say quickly. His gaze rakes over my body as it does every time we're in the same room. His appraisal makes my blood run cold, my chest constrict.

"Then get the fuck on," he snaps before turning and heading for the curtain again.

Fiona lets out a breath. "You're going to get your nuts cut off, Apollo."

"He can try," my partner replies. The bravado is false. Apollo knows our owner will not hesitate to kill him. We're disposable to the Ringmaster, each and every one of us merely toys in his game. Performers in his circus.

And if my time here has taught me anything, it's that there is no shortage in supernaturals needing a place to go.

"Let's get this over with." Apollo stands and presses his hand to my lower back. The contact is innocent, but I move away from him quickly. It took me a year before I could perform with anyone without vomiting. It hurts—to know that I will likely never get to experience physical intimacy again.

Ernesto saw to that when he broke me. Something I will not allow to happen again.

Mind on the performance ahead, I make my way up the stairs and through the curtain. The lights are bright as they shine down at Thomas and Jenny. Thomas, a wolf shifter, chases Jenny, a kitsune, around the ring. She manages to sneak past him then proceeds to leap from button to button, sending an array of glitter shooting at him until he stands before her, covered head to toe in bright red.

The crowd erupts with laughter.

We continue ascending the metal stairs until we

reach the top where Uma offers a wave and smile. Once I reach the edge of the railing where my lyra awaits, tied to a pole, I look down to watch the remainder of the 'cat and mouse' type performance.

Jenny and Thomas jump down behind boxes. When they emerge again, they're both wearing bright red jumpsuits. With a bow, they flip back behind the boxes and disappear through a trapdoor shielded behind them.

The big top is plunged into darkness save a handful of dim lights aimed at the ceiling.

I grip my lyra.

"Good luck, partner. I'll be right behind you." Apollo winks and then waits for me to climb inside. I sit on it as though it's a chair, and he releases me.

Time to shine.

The end of our show passes quickly, and soon, I'm moving as fast as I can toward the exit. People are chatting as they leave the stands, though their words all blur together as background noise.

Until— "Liv!"

I stiffen at an unfamiliar female voice calling my name. Slowly, I turn, fear crashing down on me. The only people who would know my name are those who knew me through him. My past, my monster, my nightmare.

The woman positions herself in the stands just beside my exit. Her hair is long, the dark brown strands loose around her face. She wears all black–jeans, T-shirt, and even a black lace choker adorns her neck.

A tall, raven-haired man looms behind her, his slate-gray eyes not missing anything as he guards her.

The woman opens her hand, and a copper penny dangles from a chain she holds.

My heart stops, emotion churning in my gut. I thought I'd lost it that day in the alley. That I'd never see the trinket again. I glance over at the Ringmaster, who is watching me intently. With his eyes on me, I'm confident enough to cross the distance and stop just on this side of the barrier separating us from them.

"Where did you find that?" I question, eyeing the necklace in her hand.

She gives me a mysterious smile. "It belongs to you, does it not?"

Her voice is soft, but the power radiating from her tingles across my skin, making me even more wary. Someone with this much power should be off leading a House, not here in No Man's Land.

Her focus shifts to the Ringmaster. "Just as you currently belong to him."

The man at her side is now focused purely on the Ringmaster, but I don't miss the way his hand hovers beside the woman's arm as if he'd step between her and danger in a heartbeat. What love must one feel to be willing to trade their life for someone else's?

The Ringmaster's glare hardens, his face morphing to an expression just short of deadly. I know that wrapping this conversation up quickly is in my best interest, but I cannot even begin to fathom how she came across my necklace, nor how she knew it was mine. And I am desperate to know the answers to both of those questions.

I turn back to find her leaning toward me, her eyes boring into me, the power I feel around her only growing stronger. "Don't be afraid," she says, her voice even softer as she holds the necklace out to me. "Take back what you lost."

The weight of her words settles on my shoulders as though she's telling me to take back more than just the necklace. But I shake off the thought. Nothing more belongs to me. My freedom is gone, my life owned. This heirloom is all I have to take. To possess.

Reaching out, I close my hand around the penny.

She releases it, a smile touching her lips as she gently exhales, and I'm surprised to realize she was holding her breath. Then, she glances up at the man beside her, the trust in her eyes far too pure to belong in a place like No Man's Land.

The pair quickly turns away, heading into the crowd. Within seconds, they'll disappear, so I take a chance to call out softly, uncertain if she'll hear me. "Who are you?"

The woman pauses. She glances back across her shoulder. "I'm Emmaline."

With one final smile, she and the man with her disappear into the crowd. I stare down at the penny in my hand, joy surging through me.

"Who was that?"

I stiffen, the Ringmaster's presence behind me both

unwelcome and secure. I'm at war with myself when I'm around him. A battle raging between my mind knowing I should be terrified of him even if my body is more than willing to trust him with the last remaining pieces of my soul.

○ ○ ○

To read more, get your copy of Slay Me.

In No Man's Circus, the Ringmaster controls everything—even me.

Every evening, I'm forced to perform. High above a crowd of supernaturals, I fly on my lyra. Never high enough to escape my captor.

And when the lights go down and the audience goes home, it's just him and me.

I shouldn't enjoy it.

This obsession he has with me.

But as a hybrid in a world where power is king, I'm nothing special.

Except when his eyes are on my body.

He's a beast whose strength is unparalleled, a creature who demands my obedience, but even as the twisted parts of me are drawn to him, I refuse to be broken.

He'll have to kill me first.

Get your copy here.

ALSO BY EVERLY FROST

SOUL BITTEN SHIFTER - COMPLETE

(Dark Urban Fantasy Romance)

1. This Dark Wolf

2. This Broken Wolf

3. This Caged Wolf

4. This Cruel Blood

SUPERNATURAL LEGACY - COMPLETE

(Angels and Dragon Shifters)

1. Hunt the Night

2. Chase the Shadows

3. Slay the Dawn

DEMON PACK - COMPLETE

(Dark Paranormal Romance)

1. Demon Pack

2. Demon Pack: Elimination

3. Demon Pack: Eternal

ASSASSIN'S MAGIC - COMPLETE

(Urban Fantasy Romance)

About the Author

Everly Frost is the USA Today Bestselling author of YA and New Adult urban fantasy and paranormal romance novels. She spent her childhood dreaming of other worlds and scribbling stories on the leftover blank pages at the back of school notebooks. She lives in Brisbane, Australia with her husband and two children.

amazon.com/author/everlyfrost

facebook.com/everlyfrost

twitter.com/everlyfrost

instagram.com/everlyfrost

bookbub.com/authors/everly-frost

goodreads.com/everlyfrost